MW00654074

GREED IN PARADISE

PARADISE SERIES, BOOK 5

DEBORAH BROWN

GREED IN PARADISE
Copyright @ 2014 by Deborah Brown

Excerpt from Revenge in Paradise @2014 by Deborah Brown

Published by: Paradise Books June 2014

Cover: Natasha Brown

ISBN-13: 978-0-9903166-2-6
ISBN-10: 0990316629

PARADISE SERIES NOVELS

GREED IN PARADISE

Chapter 1

I leaned back and breathed in the fresh scent of the rain that beat relentlessly on the tin roof overhead, bringing welcome relief from the heat. The walkways were puddled with water. Looking for any excuse to avoid the paperwork in front of me, I stared at the inlet that ran along the back of Jake's bar. Since buying Jake out, I evicted the roaches and became the owner of my very own dive bar. We served the best Mexican food and margaritas in town, which were two of my personal favorites.

My new routine consisted of showing up to the bar every morning to check shipments in and organize receipts from the previous day. Rain or shine, I could be found sitting at the corner table on the deck enjoying my coffee. A dreary, gray day outside was a good excuse to turn on the white Christmas lights that wrapped around the railings, the roof overhang, and flickered in the palm trees.

It surprised me to hear heavy footsteps coming up the back stairs. Jake's wasn't even open yet. Even the hardcore drunks were still asleep, and we still had another few hours before the lunch drinkers arrived.

A man with several days' worth of facial hair, mean slits for eyes, and dark hair standing on end appeared at the top of the stairs. A chill rolled up my spine.

"We're closed." I tried to smile.

"Hands up," he said as he whipped his gun from behind his back. "Now!"

Furious at myself for leaving my Glock in the nightstand next to the bed, I said, "I'm sure we can work something out without anyone ending up hurt or dead."

"Twenty-five thousand and I'll be on my way." His eyes flitted around and, popping his head inside, he saw the bar was empty. He screamed desperation.

"We don't keep that kind of money on the premises. I can give you about a thousand dollars," I said, my voice calm; it wasn't the first time I'd had a gun stuck in my face. If I was able to get the safe open, a loaded Beretta sat inside.

"Jake owes my boss and I'm here to collect." He shook his gun at me. "I know he always has piles of cash on the premises."

Damn Jake.

"He's no longer the owner and I don't run anything illegal out of here." Jake had run out of town, knowing he'd been marked as a dead man over his non-existent repayment plan for his massive gambling debt. A few other attempts at collection had been made by other gun-toting thugs, but I'd been able to convince them that the bar was under new management and they went away quietly.

"Get up, let's go and check out that safe of yours. You'd better be lying about not having cash. Boss man is tired of waiting on payment that is long overdue."

I stood up.

"Why me? I'm not Jake." After being on the run for months, Jake had finally made contact and I bought out my silent partner. We used our shared CPA to construct a fair deal and he helped me set up private, legal financing. I had several illegal options, but passed.

"Bet you'll find the money if I tie you to a chair and listen to you scream while I slice off various body parts. How many will it take, one, two…?" He whipped a blade from his back pocket, kissing it tenderly and shoving it in the front of his pants.

The chilling, matter-of-fact way he threatened me scared me more than his gun. Out of the corner of my eye, I saw Phil, the bartender, drop behind the bar. I hoped she had the sheriff on speed dial.

"Just know that if you touch me, Jimmy Spoon will track your ass down and kill you. You do know Spoon don't you?" I asked.

Jimmy Spoon was *the* badass of the Keys and claimed boyfriend status with my mother. He was reformed from his criminal days, but still inspired fear amongst the low-life element. I also knew this man would die a slow death if Spoon got ahold of him, but I stayed focused on getting out of this alive and with no missing body parts.

He laughed. "Get moving."

As I moved slowly across the wooden floor inside, he knocked me in my lower back with his gun, and I felt hot pain spidering up my back. I reflexively turned, jumped, and kicked him in the arm. When he dropped his gun and scrambled to retrieve it, I hopped to my feet and headed for the door, where I tripped.

"Damn."

Phil popped up from behind the bar and racked her shotgun. "Drop the gun, asshole." Thankfully, Jake left behind his Mossberg when he split town.

The man snaked his fingers out and, pulling his gun back into his grasp, rolled onto his back. He pointed

3

the barrel toward Phil, but she pulled her trigger first. There was blood everywhere from a gaping stomach wound and he lifted slightly off the floor just before he died.

I leapt up, "Are you okay?" I fished my cell phone from my pocket to call Kevin Cory, a local sheriff. I only had his number because his sister, Julie, was dating my brother, Brad.

"You never call, what's up?" Kevin asked when he answered.

"There's been a shooting at Jake's. No need for an ambulance; call the coroner." I wouldn't tell Kevin this, but I was glad the shooter had been dispatched to the afterlife, or he'd get out of jail and be back.

"Who'd you shoot this time?" Kevin asked. "Don't touch anything, we're on our way."

I hung up abruptly before he started to lecture. I'd tell him we must have gotten disconnected when I saw him. "I'll be upset if you quit over this," I said to Phil, taking a seat at the bar.

Curvy, blonde Phil, short for Philipa, had walked into the bar one day wanting to be the new bartender. A straight A second-year law school student, she was good for business in her butt-cheek baring jean shorts, tank tops, and tennis shoes. She handled the overly-obnoxious in an efficient manner; she'd had to ban a couple of men permanently.

"My daddy didn't raise no quitter." She laid the shotgun on the bar. "Wait till I call him tonight and give him the grisly details, he'll be bragging to his friends. Hell, he taught me and my brother to shoot—refused to have a helpless girl for a daughter."

4

Tarpon Cove is a small town that sits at the top of the Florida Keys, so the sheriff could get from one end of town to the other in a matter of minutes, depending on tourist traffic. Sirens could be heard in the distance.

"We'll need to close today," I sighed.

"I'll put out a sign: 'Death in the restaurant.' There's an upside—dirtbag's death could bring in the gawker crowd and it'll be good for business."

Phil grabbed two waters and shoved one across to me. "What did he want anyway?"

"Jake owed him money." I downed half my water, twisting the cap back on and rolling it across the back of my neck. "Maybe I need to put up a big neon sign that says, 'New owner.'"

"I've had a few collectors in here. Explained to them in small words that Jake left town, comped them a beer, and they left."

My hair clip snapped in half when I rolled on the floor, so I scooped my long red hair off my neck and fashioned it into a makeshift ponytail.

Kevin and his partner, Johnson, rushed through the door, two paramedics with a stretcher right behind them. "They don't listen very well. I told them the dude was dead," I said to Phil.

"Madison Westin, you're nothing but trouble, aren't you?" Johnson eyed me with his tight-ass smile firmly in place.

Johnson was the most uptight sheriff on the force and he even looked the part. We had a well-documented dislike for one another. It frustrated him that I never gave him an excuse to cuff me and drag me to jail.

"He walked in, pointed a gun in my face,

5

demanded money, and threatened to cut off body parts. Phil saved my life. End of story," I said.

Phil walked around the bar, extended her hand to Johnson. "Philipa Grey." She turned to me. "I advise you to call your lawyer before answering any more of the officer's questions, since there seems to be animosity between the two of you."

"Is that all you have—annoying, snotty-ass friends?" Johnson glared.

Kevin cut in. "I'll question these two, Johnson. You make sure the paramedics don't screw up the evidence. Jake's is closed today."

While Johnson stomped away, I gave the middle finger to his back. Kevin slapped my hand down and shook his head. Kevin had two personalities. Personally, I liked the out-of-uniform, easy-going, laughing, beach-boy good looks Kevin. Johnson turned back. "Madison, sorry to hear your boyfriend left you for that beautiful Italian model."

I sucked in my breath, but ignored Johnson. "Would you like something cold to drink?" I asked Kevin as I walked behind the bar.

Kevin nodded. He questioned Phil and I separately and took very few notes. He looked bored. "Dead guy is Carlos Osa—long, violent rap sheet. Good riddance."

"When can we reopen, capitalize on the bad publicity?" I asked.

"Once we haul his body out of here, we'll be done with our investigation. Pretty cut-and-dried," Kevin said. "I've got a crime scene cleaner on speed dial."

"I used him once at The Cottages. He did a good

job; you wouldn't know the stain was blood unless someone told you." I owned a ten-unit building on the beach that had seen more than its fair share of excitement.

"Try being nice to Johnson, he'll come around," Kevin said.

"I'll bake cookies," I said, struggling not to make another inappropriate gesture. "I'm going to send everyone home and I'll be out on the deck until you're done."

Chapter 2

I pushed the gas pedal of my SUV as I raced home from Jake's. All I wanted was a long, hot shower. I raced upstairs into my bathroom to stand under the rainfall showerhead, using mango body wash to ease the stress of the day. My first choice would be to crawl under my clean, soft sheets, pulling them over my head. Instead, I rooted around in my closet for something to wear to dinner. It would serve Mother right if I climbed into my ultimate comfort clothes: ankle-length sweats and a T-shirt. The only thing stopping me was the long and tortuous lecture that would follow.

Mother called with a dinner invitation and I ran several excuses through my mind before, finally, flat-out refusing. Of course, she'd been prepared and pulled out the guilt card. Beyond irritated, but resisting total defeat, I demanded we go to my favorite restaurant, The Crab Shack. She sounded excited and happy, which consumed me with guilt after we hung up. I wished that I'd been more gracious and just agreed from the beginning. I temporarily forgot Madeline Westin doesn't take no for an answer.

I threw a tropical-print slip dress onto the bed, followed by a hot pink bra. I didn't go out without cleavage. I'd outgrown my totally braless phase, saving it for lazy days.

I couldn't wait for Mother to say, "How was your

day, honey?"

"Started out with a gun in my face, but no worries, he's dead."

Since it rained all day, my long red hair bushed out to five times its normal size. I managed to tame most of it with a black pāua shell hairclip, tendrils falling around the sides of my cheeks and the back of my neck. I threw on my dress, reached for the bamboo bracelets Mother and I found in an out-of-the-way store in Marathon Key, fastened my earrings, and slipped into my flip-flops. Admiring my outfit in the standing mirror, I reluctantly chose low-heeled slip-ons because I knew Mother would freak.

Before leaving, I nuzzled the neck of my very old, longhaired, black cat, Jazz, who was laying sound asleep on my bed. His meow sounded like, "Stop that." I was damn jealous I wasn't lying beside him and it irritated me that he went right back to sleep—I could never do that so quickly.

I listened at the top of the stairs and there wasn't a single sound except for the whir of the ceiling fans. Fabiana Merceau, my best friend and roommate, had gone somewhere with her French model boyfriend, Didier. Just one name, like a rock star. He looked like one, too. He had Mother, Fab, and I under his spell.

I had inherited my two-story Key West-style home from my aunt Elizabeth. I decorated it beachy, and chose oversized down-filled furniture one could curl up on and go to sleep. I loved that family and friends knew they could choose my house to hang up their flip-flops anytime, day or night. Close friends walked in through the French doors from the patio whether they were locked or not. I tried to think of a single friend I had who didn't carry a lock pick.

Grabbing my purse off the entry bench, I went out and slid behind the wheel of my black convertible Hummer. I'd gotten an excellent deal after my previous SUV went to car heaven or was more likely smooshed and sent to a recycler after it had been torched. The streets of The Cove were slick and wet from the rain that had finally stopped. I drove slowly, which suited me anyway. I knew where all the cop hiding places were for ticket-giving, and in the long run, it was faster to drive the speed limit than to endure a cop's lecture while trying to maintain a somewhat-pleasant look while being ticketed.

A car leaving The Crab Shack left an open space for me by the front door. The fun restaurant centered around an enormous tiki bar and waterfront dining that overlooked the cooler blue water of the Atlantic, and its food never disappointed.

If I ordered wine I wouldn't be tempted to gulp it down; I just needed to take the edge off my nerves. I spotted Mother at a window table with her boyfriend, Jimmy Spoon. Both were seated so they could survey the comings and goings. To put it bluntly, Spoon looked like a thug with his scruffy brown hair and hard-as-nails brown eyes; but if you knew him, you also knew he had a huge heart. He told me once, "Don't screw me and you won't end up dead."

Mother stood and hugged me. "You look great, honey." She looked over my entire outfit down to my shoes. "Doesn't she, Spoon?" Spoon winked and pulled out my chair.

"What did you do today?" Mother asked.

"Spent most of the day at Jake's." I wasn't in the mood to relive all of the details, after all. She'd be mad when she found out. Spoon looked at me and arched his eyebrow. No wonder he hadn't said a word, he already knew and hadn't said anything either. I would have bet he knew minutes after the shooting, since the man had connections to gossip as soon as it happened. Hopefully, the doghouse would fit two.

"I'll have some white wine," I told the waiter.

Mother entwined her fingers with Spoon's, smiling at him. Good thing my brother, Brad, wasn't here. He hadn't embraced the idea of Mother being with a younger man, which I suspected didn't bother him as much as the bad-boy tag. She looked happy. She'd grown out her traditional blonde bob, which now looked wind-whipped, and the hemline of her black spaghetti-strap dress kept getting shorter. Her eyes were glued to the front of the restaurant.

"Are you expecting someone else?" I asked.

"Madeline, sorry I'm late." A man I'd never seen before appeared from out of nowhere and kissed Mother's cheek.

Spoon didn't knock him on his butt, so I assumed he knew him until he checked the man over briefly, looking amused.

"This is my daughter, Madison Westin." She smiled at him, then me. "Brian Varner," she introduced. Brian held out his hand.

"I've been looking forward to dinner," he said politely.

"I don't shake hands."

I found that nicety to be completely abhorrent;

who knew where his hands had been? Mother kicked me under the table while Brian mumbled something and sat down next to me. I looked at Spoon's face and knew Mother had once again broken her promise and set me up.

Mother and her damned blind dates...not one of them had ever been remotely interesting. I had a reprieve while Zach and I were a couple, but since I was single again, she wouldn't rest until I was married and her dream of grandchildren came true. She stopped pestering Brad with attempts at fix-ups once he began dating Julie. She had a son named Liam, giving Mother one almost-grandchild; and she salivated for more.

I turned to Brian. "So, you're my date?" The waiter set my wine glass in front of me or I'd have left.

He looked like a nice guy, but what did that mean anyway? Boring! A non-descript fellow, brown hair, cheeks flushed. I'd bet one of his body parts that he had no clue what he was getting into.

He groaned. "I'm sorry you didn't know."

"Brian is the director at Sunnyside Retirement Home. We met when he filled in and conducted a tour for my poker group." Mother smiled at him.

"Are you and Spoon thinking about a move to the old-folks home?" I asked.

Brian coughed and took a drink of water. "Sunnyside is a scenic, maintenance-free, upscale senior-living retirement community, with all the amenities and extensive health care options for those in their retirement years."

"Do you have a minimum age requirement?" I asked. "He's my age," I said, and looked at Spoon.

Spoon glared at me and I gave it right back. He

downed the rest of his beer and set the bottle down with a bang.

Mother frowned. "Brian and I sat together at lunch and I realized the two of you had a lot in common. He's unattached and so are you. It's time for you to meet someone new."

Brian looked uncomfortable. "I want to thank you, Madeline, for referring the Odell's Sunnyside's way." He looked at me. "Your mother's friends are quite lively."

"They all smoke, drink, and gamble, don't let those phony chips fool you; they're backed with hard cash and payout when they leave. Do you allow these activities?" I pasted a phony smile on my face.

"Madison!" Mother kicked me again.

"We have a Bingo night that's very popular," Brian said.

I bet about now Brian wished he had ordered something besides a Shirley Temple. "My boyfriend left me for his supermodel ex-wife. What's your story?" I took my annoyance with Mother out on him, and I regretted it instantly.

He patted my hand. "Madeline told me your sad little story. I'm very sorry." He put his arm around my shoulders. "She also told me about your penchant for bad boys, they're never worth it in the end," he clucked. "You should try a regular guy for a change."

"What a prick," Spoon mouthed, glaring at him.

"I can't believe you," I said angrily to Mother. "What about your boyfriend?" I looked at Spoon. "She wasted your time," I said to Brian and pushed his arm away. I grabbed my glass of wine, downed every last drop, and slammed it onto the table, shattering the stem.

No one said a word.

I shoved my chair back. "I'm not ready." I burst into tears and ran past the hostess stand at the front of the restaurant, and right into the open arms of Creole who was coming in the door.

Chapter 3

Creole grew up down the block from my Aunt Elizabeth, whom he had enjoyed a mother-son relationship with. She had unofficially adopted him, often hiding him from an abusive, drunken father. It surprised me that my brother and I didn't meet him until I came to live in Tarpon Cove. Since my aunt's death, I learned that she lived two lives and actually managed to keep them separate. From the day Creole introduced himself to the family, Mother had opened her heart to him as if he were a second son.

He put his arm around me and led me out of the restaurant. "Why are you crying?" he growled. "You know I hate that."

"Take me home," I sniffed.

Creole scooped me up in his arms and carried me across the parking lot to his pickup truck. He reached into the glove box and handed me a napkin after depositing me on the front seat.

"Do I need to go back in there and beat the hell out of someone?" His crystal blue eyes, now dark cobalt, bore into me.

I hit the highlights of what Mother had done and also explained that I overreacted because I'd had a crappy day.

"Madeline and I need to have talk. I'll make it very clear that when you're ready, I'm going to be your first date," he barked.

It didn't take long for Creole to become firmly entrenched as a member of our family—but thankfully not elated by blood, since we'd kissed more than once. Even though he was easy to look at, lean and hard, and moved like a tiger on the prowl, I had no plans to start dating when breaking up still felt like an open wound. Besides, there were a few black marks on my relationship track record; an ex-husband lurked around out there somewhere.

"I'm high maintenance. I've been called crazy more times than I can count, and I've been known to carry a gun." I smiled at him.

"You threatened to shoot me once, and did you see me running for the door?"

My stomach growled loudly. A glass of white wine on an empty stomach was now making me nauseous.

"How about Roscoe's?" he asked. "I can get us onto the secret back patio where all the tables have chairs."

Roscoe's served the best burgers in Tarpon Cove, but after a couple of fights broke out he removed all of the seating in the front and told people to eat in their car or leave. He didn't have a brisk walk-up business but the drive-through always had a waiting line. He could afford to reject the "customers always comes first" rule.

"Afterward, I need to go back to The Crab Shack and get my SUV." I grabbed another napkin and wiped my eyes.

Creole picked up his phone. "Madison's car is in the parking lot; you make sure it gets back to her place. It's the least you can do since you're part of the reason I found her crying." After a short pause he added, "And tell your girlfriend that the next time she wants to set Madison

16

up on a date, she runs it by me first. Got that?" He sat listening for a minute and then hung up.

"How did Spoon take you telling him what to do?"

"He laughed at my nerve but said he'd get your SUV back to the house. He can't shoot me, I'm law enforcement."

Shortly after my aunt's death, Creole came back to South Florida on loan from the DEA in the pursuit of a big drug case. After locking up the bad guys, he transferred permanently to the Miami office and now consorts with drug dealers all day. "Creole" is an alias for his undercover work. Only a handful of people know his real name—Luc Baptiste. The Westin family perfected the art of secret keeping.

He pulled into Roscoe's and parked. "Don't move."

He favored the big testosterone trucks, and being short made it impossible for me to get in and out by myself in a dignified fashion. He opened the door. I held out my arms and he swung me onto the ground, gave me a shake, and pushed me up against the side of his truck.

"You will explain to me why you didn't call me after the shooting at Jake's, and how come I had to hear about it through the grapevine." Turning me completely around, he said, "No bandages, that's a good sign." He leaned down, his lips grazing my cheek.

He tugged on my hand, clearly impatient, and hustled me around the back and in through the delivery entrance. Roscoe and Creole did a convoluted hand shake, and man-hugged. Creole introduced me, saying, "This is Madison, my next girlfriend."

Roscoe gave a shout of laughter before his dark eyes swept over me from head to toe. He stood basketball player tall, towering over Creole who is well over six feet. "Nice to meet you." He smiled his approval. "I suppose you want entre to the private patio?"

"Can I brag to my friends?" I asked. I had enjoyed Roscoe's food on many occasions. It was the place to go when your mouth watered for a great hamburger, but I always had to enjoy them from the front seat of my SUV.

Roscoe shook his finger. "No, you cannot. The riffraff will converge and demand entrance." He took our order and I noticed he stuck it first on the wheel.

Creole pulled out my chair and went and got us bottled water. "Look at me," he said when he returned, sitting across the small table from me. "You didn't call me or Fab, why not?"

"Do you want me to cry all through dinner?" I flashed him a sad face, hoping to change the subject.

"I can get the information out of you and there won't be a single tear shed." He twisted my hair around his fingers and pulled my face forward. "Start talking."

"Started the morning with being threatened. He's dead; left a big mess. Johnson the sheriff is a dick and the crime scene cleaner dude is seriously weird. Can't believe Kevin tried to fix up his sister Julie with him. Why were you at The Crab Shack?"

"Harder called with some sketchy details but knew you'd come out without a scratch. I went by the house and Fab informed me you were at The Crab Shack having dinner with Mother. She said Madeline stopped by, acting weird, so I thought I'd better check it out."

Harder had earned the esteemed title of Chief of

18

Detectives for the illustrative Miami police department, and was Creole's boss. We got off to a rocky start, when he thought I had criminal tendencies and I thought he was an ass. Turns out we were both wrong.

I asked Harder once, "What's your first name?"

"Detective," he said. Now I suppose he'd change it to "Chief."

Creole cut into my thoughts. "I heard Johnson had a few choice words for you today. He won't bother you again. Ever," he assured me.

Johnson, the newest member of the sheriff's department, would laugh off threats of bodily harm. Best case scenario, he gets transferred to Boise.

I changed the subject. "How was your day, honey?"

He put his lips to mine. "I could get used to you asking me that question."

One of the cooks came out and set our hamburgers—loaded with lettuce, tomatoes, pickles, and secret sauce—and little skinny fries in front of us. "I love their fries." I popped one into my mouth.

Creole watched me devour the French fry. "I had a high-level meeting this morning and then went back to the office for a long, boring conference call. Harder and I started throwing paper balls at one another. He taped the call so his assistant can get us a transcript by morning."

"Did I say thank you for rescuing me from a dreadful evening?" I looked at his flawless caramel-colored skin and shoulder-length dark hair. I wanted to fling myself in his arms, but not while still second-guessing my previous relationship, which felt like a failure on par with my divorce. "You're smoking hot. You deserve someone not on the rebound; a woman who makes you laugh and serves you breakfast, or coffee anyway, in bed."

He lifted my chin and looked into my eyes. "You have a little time left to decide you want me on your own. After that, I'm going to pursue you relentlessly until you change your mind."

"That sounds stalkerish."

Creole tightened his grip on my chin. "Tell me you feel nothing when we kiss, that my fingers on your skin leaves you cold. Tell me to get lost and I will."

We stared at one another. "No matter what happens, I'm never going to tell you to get lost."

He picked up a French fry and shoved it between my lips.

Chapter 4

Fab stomped into the kitchen, yelling, her blue eyes glaring. "I will not allow you to turn into a crappy friend." She grabbed me and ran her hand across my back. "Go get your Glock, right now."

"He's dead. That should make you happy." I reached for my favorite coffee mug, white ceramic with raised seashells.

It annoyed me that Fab always managed to look great in the morning with relatively no primping. Her waist-length brown hair tied up in a ponytail, she had on her favorite skinny jeans and a white, low cut T-shirt, which camouflaged her Walther at the small of her back.

Fab, a coffee snob, got her special blend out of the refrigerator. If you asked me, it looked like mud and the first sip made you gag.

She snapped her fingers at me. "I hate that Zach made you doubt yourself. If you don't snap out of it, I will hurt you."

"How will you explain that to Mother?" I smirked. "Did you know what she had planned at dinner last night?" My eyes narrowed.

"What I know is I had to hear from Creole that you almost died yesterday. The only thing that made me happy was that he had to hear the news from Harder," she snickered. "What did Madeline do now?"

Fab and Harder had an avid dislike for each other.

21

He itched to arrest her, and he knew her investigation skills blurred the lines of legality, but she still managed to elude his grasp.

"She fixed me up with some bland piece of toast, forgot his name already. Can you imagine the first kiss when he feels up my Glock?" I half laughed. "Creole said he'd make sure she doesn't do that again."

"What's up with you two? The way he looks at you should make you want to get naked."

"He did mention he could use my body in delightful ways to wipe every memory of Zach from my mind and heart." The thought of being horizontal with an unrestrained Creole made my skin tingle.

"What's wrong with you? He's almost as hot as my Didier. What is it that disgusts you? The rock hard abs, tight ass, or those long legs that could wrap double around your frame? He speaks French, so he can whisper those naughty things you like to hear."

Didier had spoiled me and Mother, always whispering French in our ears, eliciting blushes and giggles. He flirted shamelessly, and we loved every second.

"Just like I yelled at Mother last night in the middle of the restaurant, I'm not ready."

Fab poured herself some coffee and sat at the island. "Sorry I missed that scene. How are you two going to make up?"

"I'm not speaking to her today so I have time to come up with something."

We clinked coffee mugs and laughed.

Zach walked by the kitchen window, not looking in. It had recently been replaced with a garden window

22

and filled with small tropical plants. The last hail storm that blew through targeted the panes, causing cracks. Now we had a larger view of the entire front of the house and anyone who walked through the gate.

"Hand me the gun in the drawer." Fab held out her hand. "I'll get rid of him and explain what no trespassing means."

Past experience taught us that a Beretta in the utensil drawer could come in handy.

Zach Lazarro owned AZL, a security firm that boasted individual and corporate clients. Slice, his right-hand man, recently became a partner and the two traveled in a pack. Slice put his hands to the window, looking in, and waved. The doorbell rang.

Fab slid off the stool and was half way to the door. She cracked the door open, sticking her nose out, and said, "What?"

I couldn't hear what was said, but Fab looked at me and I nodded to let them in.

Zach and Slice filled the kitchen; both were over six feet tall, ex-navy seals, and hard-asses. Slice was a species all to himself. Over two hundred pounds, he was a solid wall of steel, complete with a menacing scar that ran the entire length of his face.

"You made me coffee." Slice bared his teeth at Fab, his version of a smile.

Zach hugged me. "Came to check on you. I heard about yesterday."

I wanted to run my hands through his tousled black hair and smooth it down. "Help yourself to something to drink. I'm considering a name change for Jake's, and in the meantime, I'm putting up a sign shouting new ownership."

Zach grabbed a bottle of water from the fridge and slid onto a stool across from me at the island. His blue eyes were intense, checking me over. Slice grabbed Fab's elbow and lead her out to the patio. She'd be mad that he cut off her eavesdropping opportunity.

"Jake's not coming back," I told Zach. "I bought him out and it's all legal-like."

He covered my hands with his. "I'm sorry about how everything went down between us. You deserved to find out from me and not to be publically embarrassed."

He had been my boyfriend since shortly after I arrived in Tarpon Cove. After a long relationship of I save your life, you save mine, I met his parents for the first time in a restaurant, along with his ex-wife, Lucia, and son, Anthony III—Zach looking uncomfortable to acknowledge our relationship. Thank goodness for Mother and Creole; they got me out of there with my dignity intact.

He continued. "Lucia showed up on my parent's doorstep with her luggage and our son. Anthony had begun asking questions about his father, and she didn't want to compound her lies by saying I'd died."

"That must have been a shock for your parents." I'd already heard bits and pieces of the hows and whys and, quite frankly, I didn't want to hear anymore. At the time of Lucia's arrival, our relationship had begun to crack under the stress of what he termed my being a "Fab wannabe." Earlier that day, he told me he needed a break in the relationship. He wanted a stay-at-home girlfriend, not one who carried a gun and partnered with Fab on her quasi-legal jobs.

"Lucia found out she was pregnant after the divorce became final. She figured I wouldn't be interested since we had an acrimonious divorce. We've talked through our issues and we're considering reconciliation, but our focus is Anthony."

This was the first time he had stopped by since that fateful night, although I'd seen glimpses of him around town. I supposed it was nice for him to stop by and check on me, but I wanted to tell him not to do it again. "I'm happy for you; I know you wanted a family." I smiled, although I know it never made it to my eyes. "You look rested and relaxed."

He squeezed my hand.

Do I look happy? Look rested and relaxed? No, I don't. I wanted to tell him to get out of my house. I couldn't fault him; he did what any man with integrity would do, stand by his child and the child's mother. That's why I had loved him.

"I want us to be friends." His blue eyes searched my face. "I hope you'll call if you ever need anything. You are the first woman to drag me out of my cave and make me laugh at myself."

On the verge of crying, I picked up my mug and put it in the sink. I needed a distraction from his scrutiny. We'd both been instilled with good manners, so it was a given we'd always be pleasant to one another. Hopefully I never ran into his new family. "I'd like that; your number is still on speed dial."

Zach checked his watch. "We've got a meeting to get to at the office." He walked around the island and pulled me into a hug.

Slice must have positioned his chair so that he

could see inside the French doors from the patio to the kitchen. He and Fab walked back in as if on cue. Slice picked me up off my feet in a bear hug. "Call me."

When I didn't respond, he squeezed me hard. I grunted, "Okay, already."

Fab and I sat in silence and watched them leave, hearing the truck doors slam.

My cell phone rang and Fab grabbed it off the counter and handed it to me. I listened and said, "Fab and I are on our way." I hung up. "Gus Ivers died and Tolbert needs company."

Fab held out the car keys. "Would you like to drive?"

I laughed and reached out and touched her forehead. "My own SUV? Since I've been busy feeling sorry for myself, your crappy driving doesn't bother me as much."

Chapter 5

We bumped over the gravel road into The Wild Bird Farm and under the cement overhang to the driveway, which was home to hundreds of varieties of wild green parrots with varied-colored underbellies. Fab blew down the road, making it in record time; she had the two-lane Overseas Highway mostly to herself. It wasn't until another driver wanted to use a piece of her road that horns honked and fingers waved.

Once we parked, Grover, a Golden Retriever, ran to meet us. He had lived with me for a while; I rescued and nursed him back to health. Eventually, I located and returned him to his owner. He hadn't forgotten me and a lapping dog kiss was just what the doctor ordered.

Tall and lean, Tolbert Rich stood on the porch of his old, rambling plantation-style home. The large property boasted one hundred-year-old willow and oak trees, a pond that had recently been home to an alligator until it wandered off, and an assortment of children's toys. The toys belonged to his grandchildren, who lived with him full-time since the death of their father.

I chose the wicker bench because Grover could sit next to me. Fab hugged Tolbert and they whispered to one another. She had grown as attached to him as she had to Mother. A tired wicker serving tray sat on the table; today it held a pitcher of raspberry and strawberry water. Someone had shared the recipe with him and now every

27

time we visited he found new fruit for a different flavor to try. I picked up a cookie and shared half with Grover, who had already put his head on my lap.

Tolbert sat opposite me and ran his fingers through his full head of white hair. "Gus wasn't that old in the scheme of life. He recently had a doctor's appointment and got a clean bill of health and goes home and dies?" Gus and Tolbert were close in age, both in their seventies.

"Did the sheriff suspect foul play?" I asked. "Do you?" I grabbed two more pillows. The wicker furniture had character, but wasn't all that comfortable without cushioning.

"The coroner deemed it 'natural causes,' pending toxicology reports. Gus went to bed and never woke up." Tolbert poured himself some tea. "I hadn't heard from him in a couple of days and went over there and saw his car in the driveway. I beat on the door and got no response, and the doors were locked. I got the key from the planter and went in, the smell alerted me that he'd died before I found him and confirmed for myself."

"Gus was a crusty old thing." Fab patted Tolbert's shoulders. "Anyone want him dead?"

"I guess I'm just being silly. He died in his sleep, no pain, no suffering, and he's in a better place." Tolbert held her hand.

"Who inherits his estate?" I asked. The answer would put that person at the top of a suspect list if there were to be questions.

"His daughter, Violet. Those two locked horns recently over some business dealings. It upset Gus that she had been digging into his financial affairs and knew details that he clearly had no intention of sharing, as he thought they were none of her business. He couldn't figure out how she managed to get her hands on his private information. Then she started to make threats about taking him to court for conservatorship. He wasn't out of his mind."

"Conservatorship? She'd have to prove him mentally incompetent and have doctors concur. How did she plan to hop that hurdle?" I asked.

"At first, Gus laughed it off. But I know it worried him because she seemed to know more about the process than made him comfortable, and quite confidant she would be doing what was in his best interest."

"Depending on the judge's order, she could've potentially controlled every facet of his life. Did he show signs of dementia?" I asked.

"Gus did the numbers puzzle every day in the newspaper," Fab sniffed.

I raised my eyebrows. "How do you know?"

"He showed up here every time I came to visit. He'd sit his butt in the chair over there and complain that he couldn't hear out of that crappy hearing aid of his. Maybe that's why Violet thought he was losing it. I had to yell at him; with all his money, he took cheap to a new level."

"That's so sweet of you to yell at an old man," I said.

Tolbert laughed. "Fab has a way with us older men."

"How the hell else could he hear me? Last visit, I told him I'd go to lunch, but only if he could hang on my every word without having to ask, 'What?'"

I reached for another cookie and shared it with

Grover, who lifted his head.

"That's not allowed," Tolbert said pointing at the cookie crumbs.

"You know, I feel the same way when Fab feeds my cat, Jazz, bologna treats. And she ignores me every time."

"You both are the sassiest little things." He shook his finger. "Did you know," he said to me, "I barely mentioned that the church bus took a while to start one morning and the next day, one of Mr. Spoon's employees showed up with a pickup full of tools and had it running pretty by the afternoon. How do you suppose that happened?" He looked at Fab.

Pastor Tolbert Rich operated the Church of the Traveling Jesus, a school bus that had been renovated by one of Spoon's guys, painted in patriotic colors. He picked up his parishioners on Sundays along the Keys, preached a feel good sermon, and served lunch. Far as I knew, every week he had a packed bus and no one said an unkind word.

"Doesn't matter, the important part is that it runs," I said. "You're not very good at accepting help. It will be character-building for those guys to help the nicest man in Pigeon Key."

Spoon hired recently-paroled felons, giving them a second chance. He had a high success rate; one guy in particular went into construction and I used him at Jake's and for projects around my house. It was my lucky day when I discovered the man hadn't overhyped his abilities and didn't charge "screw you" rates.

Tolbert looked at his watch. "I have to go to Tarpon Cove hospital before visiting hours end. Yesterday

I arrived late and they wouldn't let me in."

"You have to be kidding me. Did you whip out your preacher card?" I asked.

He laughed. "I'm a rule follower. I turned and left and vowed to be on time today."

Fab sucked down the last of her water. "I'll call Shirl. She's a nurse-something there and I'll tell her to be on the lookout. She owes me and will still owe me after this one."

I winked at Tolbert and put a finger to my lips so that he wouldn't lecture Fab. She got her phone out of her pocket and walked off the porch.

"Shh," I whispered to Tolbert. "Shirl is one of my tenants and loves that she 'owes' Fab. She'll be secretly thrilled to know there will be more requests in the future. Fab doesn't need to know Shirl has a severe girl crush."

"She wouldn't force someone to…" He looked worried.

"If it makes you feel better, I've shot more people than she has during our friendship."

He looked shocked and at a loss for words.

Fab interrupted, "Shirl's on duty until ten tonight. Ask for her at the nurse's station."

I stacked everything back onto the tray. "Where will the funeral for Gus be held?"

"I'm going to talk to Violet about that, I'd like to officiate. I'll let you know."

Fab hugged him. "We'll be there."

I slipped Grover another cookie and accepted a dog hug.

31

Chapter 6

We both looked at each other and said, "Tropical Slumber."

Fab flew into the driveway of the funeral home, which had once been a hot dog stand, renovated several times over the years making room for multiple additions and, most recently, a crematorium. She screeched to a halt on the red carpet; the parking lot was empty.

"At least we won't be interrupting a final send off." I looked around. "I guess I won't be grabbing a couple of those little sandwiches on the way out the door."

"They have a refrigerator full of funeral food." Fab kept her finger on the bell.

The front door pushed open and Raul stuck his head out. "Fabiana!" He smiled and pulled on a strand of her waist-length hair.

Dickie and Raul were co-owners and couldn't be more different looks wise. Raul was a dark-skinned body builder, while Dickie was a string bean and pale just-a-shade-up-from-death color.

It felt awkward to ask Raul for favors, but Dickie owed me and I him. I had gotten into the habit of collecting IOUs; advice from my Aunt Elizabeth, who said one or two in your pocket were useful. "Is Dickie busy?" I knew Dickie took pride in dressing dead people for their final bow and I wouldn't want to interrupt him.

"He's on a body run." Raul opened the door wide,

motioning us inside. "You wouldn't be here for another hand of poker, would you?" he asked Fab. "She stripped my pockets bare the last time she was here."

I sat on the bench inside the door. Fab roamed around the room. Looking into each open viewing room, she refrained from opening the closed doors with name cards. "Did you pick up Gus Ivers?" she asked.

"Last night, and he's been cremated," Raul told us. "The daughter, Violet Ivers, barked orders that we were to be waiting to escort the body of her father as soon as the coroner signed the release. Then she demanded an instant cremation. Religious reasons I assume, but didn't ask. Odd though, that she wanted to view the process. Dickie flipped, already upset his expertise wouldn't be needed. He hates cremation."

"We're just checking to make sure Gus died a natural death and was not helped by anyone." Fab finished looking around and stood by the front door, poised for a quick exit.

The waiting area was decorated in heavy ornate furniture, covered in brocade patterns, slip-covered in plastic. Not particularly comfortable, but one probably didn't stay any longer than necessary. After a while the backs of your legs stuck to the furniture, leaving a sweat spot when you stood.

"Nothing unusual," Raul said. "Death certificate said kidney failure. The coroner is a friend, so if there were irregularities he'd tell us. Gus's doctor signed off. If they suspected foul play, they wouldn't have released the body so quickly."

Astro and Necco came barreling around the corner into the reception area. One of them had a leash in its mouth, skidding to a stop. Both Dobermans, I couldn't tell them apart. The dogs lucked out; when they desperately needed a home, Dickie and Raul took them in and they had thrived.

"Thanks for the info," I said. "You and Dickie stop by Jake's any time. Spread the word—new owner."

"We both liked Jake, but have you thought about a new name?" Raul asked. "We got Carlos Osa's body. An envelope of cash arrived shortly after with instructions to bury him. Three well-dressed men in expensive black suits showed up for his farewell, looked him over, and left. Scared Dickie and I, but we tried to be cool. Not sure if we pulled it off. We triple-locked the doors when they left for whatever good that would have done. If they really wanted inside they'd shoot the locks off like I heard your friend here say once." He looked at Fab.

I couldn't muster any sympathy for Carlos. It still made me shudder to think about having my body parts sliced off.

"Maybe I'll have a name that bar contest," I joked, although I'd probably never agree to that, because I wouldn't be forced into using some dreadful name. "Your dogs are about to run out of patience. Have fun." Astro and Necco sat thumping their tails hard on the floor.

Fab waved to Raul and shot out the door, leaving me to say our good-byes. "Could Raul and Dickie be any different?" I said, climbing into the passenger side.

"Raul and I are both insomniacs. We spent late nights playing board games and talking when I hid out here. He told me he loves Dickie because he's wicked smart, they like all the same things, and he's got a gigantic—"

"Stop. La, la, la…" I covered my ears.

"I asked if it did tricks and Raul winked at me." Fab belly-laughed.

"You're so nervy." I shook my head.

"I've already got my questions lined up for when I hear the first Creole-induced screams coming from your bedroom." She continued to laugh.

My cheeks burned and I turned and stared out the window at the choppy Gulf waters, the waves pounding against the rocks. I fished my phone out of my pocket. "Hello, Mr. Harder, Detective, sir." I put him on speakerphone so that Fab wouldn't wreck trying to listen.

Fab had to know everything; she boldly snooped, eavesdropped, and had no shame. She'd stare a person down with a dare-me-to-shoot-you look on her face. It only annoyed me in that she didn't always reciprocate.

"What do you want?" he half growled.

"Tolbert Rich's best friend, Gus Ivers, just died. Cause of death is officially listed as kidney failure. Just for his peace of mind, would you have a thorough look-see at the toxicology reports when they come in?" Harder and Tolbert had become friends when he rode the church bus to catch a couple of criminals, and now he attended intermittently.

"I'll look into that and go visit Tolbert myself. Thanks for telling me about Gus."

"Tolbert could use a new best friend. I'm going to hook him up with some other old men, and you could do your part." I knew perfectly well Tolbert had twenty years on Harder.

He snorted. "I'll bring him in for free lunch at Jake's. We'll pay our respects to the murder spot. So sad, there is one less criminal no longer among us."

"Phil painted a star on the floor and it's become quite the attraction," I said.

"I'm planning on arresting Zach."

Fab and I looked at one another. I raised my eyebrow. She shook her head, indicating that it was the first she had heard the news.

"What for?"

"I'll think of something. You okay?"

Since Harder and I had forged a friendship, he'd come through for me on a couple occasions. He never liked Zach; they'd clashed once on a big case and neither got over it.

"I'm fine. If I was standing in front of you, and we were huggers, I'd think about it," I said. We both shared the same aversion for handshakes and body touching.

"You've wasted enough of my time. You and that crazy girlfriend of yours, stay out of trouble." He hung up.

"Who knew he could be human?" Fab said. "You're getting your old sparkle back."

I looked at her. "Shh, don't tell anyone. I even miss Brick a little. I'm sad I can't take the Hummer to Famosa Motors to get serviced."

"You never did tell me what happened between the two of you."

"Brick summoned me to his office. I marched in full of nerve and threw the envelope of eviction notices on his desk and told him to go to hell."

I had worked for Brick Famosa to get the hours needed for my own private investigator license. My last assignment had been to serve eviction notices on an apartment of retired seniors living on fixed incomes. He should have known that would backfire. Instead of serving the notices, I stalled for a few days and then called in a few favors to get them a pro bono lawyer who would stall the process even longer and get them relocation money.

Bitsy sat in her usual place at the receptionist desk when I cruised through the doors of Famosa Motors. The stripper-turned-receptionist looked confident. Ever since she screwed Fab by selling bad information, we'd both taken a dislike to her, knowing that she couldn't be trusted.

"He's expecting you," Bitsy said with disdain, and went back to filing her nails.

I stood inside Brick's door waiting for him to get off the phone, surveying the busy street below. I never tired of staring out his window. His office encompassed the entire second floor and had an amazing panoramic view of his luxury car lot and the surrounding area.

"Here, sign these." He pushed a stack of proof of services across the desk; he needed my signature to get the legal ball rolling.

"What in the hell made you think I'd be a part of evicting senior citizens?"

When he opened the envelope and saw they were unserved, his face tightened, his dark eyes snapping with anger. "You dare to screw me," he bellowed.

"The decent and legal thing to do would have been to hire someone to help relocate them, which they are entitled to by law. What the hell is the matter with you, the family man? Does your mother know?" I stood on the other side of his desk behind the chairs so that he couldn't grab me.

He sent the notices flying through the air. "Get the hell out of here."

I stopped and turned back. "If a single one of them ends up on the street, I'll make sure it's front page news in the Herald. Try living up to your Cuban man of the year award."

I walked by Bitsy and she had a huge smile on her face. "So sad," she purred, "that we won't be seeing you again."

"Careful, Bits, or I'll snatch that ugly blonde wig off your head and stick it in the toilet." I stepped forward, hand out.

Throwing herself out of her chair, she yelled and ran for the bathroom, locking the door.

"Sorry I missed that," Fab said.

"Yeah, well, there goes the Private Investigator license. I don't think I really wanted it anyway, just wanted to be cool like you."

Fab held out her knuckles. "You're cool, in your weird little way."

Chapter 7

Fab zipped into the driveway of The Cottages and parked in front of the office. I had inherited the property from my Aunt Elizabeth and along with it two dying tenants, Miss January and Joseph. They had both flipped the bird to their doctors, continuing to smoke and drink long past their expiration dates. Julie, my brother's girlfriend, and her son, Liam, were long-time tenants and the only normal ones.

The Cottages is a ten-unit, three-sided square, separated from the white sandy beach of the Gulf of Mexico by a wrought-iron fence. After all the construction on cottage ten was completed, you'd never know it had been burned to the ground by a meth head in pursuit of the good life, selling drugs.

I received a text from my property manager Mac Lane; new tenants were moving in today. We had a proven terrible track record when it came to scrutinizing renters, but she still ignored my edict on not renting to locals. I preferred the snowbirds from Canada and Europe, since tourists kept us booked well in advance.

Mac sat reading in the barbeque area with Shirl, another tenant. They were to the right as we drove in the driveway, with their chairs positioned so that they could scrutinize everything that happened on the property. Both were good-sized, dark-haired, curvy women who liked to stuff themselves inside clothes that were clearly too small, like the short shorts and tanks they had on now. Shirl stood and waved, bent over, and stuffed her boobs back inside her shirt. Mac pulled on a prairie-looking dress over her outfit and slipped into flip-flops with feathers attached to the tops.

"Who's that?" I pointed to a fiftyish, overly tanned blonde with large black roots and a string bikini, who cut across the driveway from the pool area to cottage seven on the end.

"That's Kathy Stone, the new tenant. She and her husband, Ron, will be living here for three months. They just sold their house, the big yellow waterfront on Pelican Avenue. They're waiting to close on their new home that's a few blocks over and in need of repairs before move-in day." Mac waved to her.

"There should be an age limit on the tag for male and female bikinis," Fab said.

I agreed with Fab. I'd seen several instances of ill-fitting bathing suits parading down the beach that made me squinch my eyes closed.

"You know my preference is tourists over tenants." Tourists tended to leave their crazy ways back in their home countries, as we tended to cater to mostly European clientele. "Did you triple check those two out?"

"Ran a background check; no criminal history. Ron's a contractor and Kathy owns Beach Chic at the Pass. They promised three months max and they paid in full; the deposit was made in cash, and I got a cashier's check for the first and last month." Mac looked proud of herself.

"I'm going down there to introduce myself, and say hello to Joseph," I said.

Shirl spoke up. "He and Svetlana are napping; he had a hard time sleeping last night."

The best exception to my rule had been Shirl. She worked at Tarpon Cove hospital and her nursing skills came in handy with Miss January and Joseph. They both liked her, sometimes making up ailments to get her attention.

Svetlana is Joseph's knockout, sexy Swedish girlfriend and they were inseparable. It takes a minute to realize she's rubber, which has a fancier name, but either way, she still has to be blown up.

"I haven't met her yet," Fab said, "but I hear she comes with a closet full of clothes."

"Twizzle, her first owner, liked to play dress-up," Shirl said. "I'm surprised he didn't request to be buried with her; they were quite close. It was thoughtful of Twizzle to will her to Joseph."

"I'll be back in a few minutes." I walked down the driveway to hold a meet-and-greet with the new tenant.

I knocked politely on the door; Kathy better hope I never had cause to use my cop knock. She peeked her head out. "Yes?"

"I wanted to introduce myself. I'm the owner, Madison Westin."

She stepped outside in a T-shirt that barely covered anything, expertly closing the door behind her, leaving no chance for a quick look. "Madison, yes I've heard all about you from your charming manager, Mac."

"I just wanted to go over a couple of rules." I smiled, despite the way she sized me up from head to toe. "If the sheriff arrives for a nuisance call, you get one freebie. The second time, you move out. No sex in the pool."

Her eyes narrowed. "I think you'll find we'll be the perfect tenants."

It didn't go unnoticed that after answering the question, she couldn't maintain eye contact. It impressed me that she appeared to listen intently and was still able to scan the driveway at the same time.

A warning chill flew up my spine. "I'd like to meet Ron, is he home?"

"My baby's asleep, he works hard," she purred, brushing her hair back. "Nice to meet you." She cracked the door open and slipped inside, closing it before I could say another word.

If I hadn't already done the crazy-tenant dance, I'd have missed the at-war body language. Her face was calm and unreadable. When she saw my close scrutiny, she hid her clenched fists behind her back, shifting from one foot to the other. I already looked forward to the day the Stones moved out.

Each cottage had a planter that ran along both sides. I walked back, noticing which ones needed more impatiens, flowers used for ground cover in the bare spots amongst the tropical plants. It didn't help when the occasional tenant, usually on the run from the law, jumped out the window and trampled them to death. Add in too much heat and no matter how hard we tried, the blossoms died anyway. The rude guy at the nursery snickered, "Nothing lives forever."

"Anything else I don't know about?" I asked Mac.

"The fun drunks across the street got evicted by the sheriff this morning and all their stuff moved out to the curb. Most of it disappeared shortly after. People are still stopping and picking through. Good thing trash day is tomorrow," Mac related.

"Stay out of trouble, you two," I said. Fab and I got into the SUV. "Take me home, I need a nap."

Chapter 8

I woke up with big plans to do absolutely nothing the entire day. I stared out the window, at my bedroom's view of the backyard. I had turned the concrete pad that surrounded the pool into a tropical oasis. My Aunt Elizabeth loved to plant all species of hibiscus and other tropical flowers, and I continued the tradition with potted plants that wrapped around the entire yard.

Desperate for coffee, I pulled on my black sweat shorts and a T-shirt. Unless Fab had awoken early, Jazz would be mad that no one filled his bowl with fresh food.

No wonder Jazz wasn't howling; when I walked into the kitchen, Didier had him on the island counter feeding him cat food. I guess the cat forgot he only liked people food. It annoyed me that Jazz didn't give everyone else the same annoying "I'm spoiled" attitude, but I bit back my words and opted for, "Good Morning." Since my coffee consisted of a mix and water, I planned for a quick getaway to sit out by the pool and leave the lovebirds to their orange juice.

Didier nodded his head. He and Fab fit together perfectly, her head nestled against his shoulder, both of them dark-haired and blue-eyed, lean and hard. The way the two of them managed to look so hot first thing in the morning irritated me, especially since this morning I looked like a wild woman just off a bender.

"Good. You're awake. I need your help today."

Fab poured herself another cup of coffee. "I need to retrieve a Mercedes for a bookie client of mine down in Key West."

I've never said no to Fab before; in fact, I rarely said no to anyone—which needed to be corrected, as far as I was concerned.

"I'm sorry, I have a busy day," I flat-out lied, and instantly regretted it.

Fab's blue eyes snapped with suspicion. "I spent yesterday driving you around being my most charming self."

"Well, maybe I'd drive myself if I could ever get my car keys away from you," I huffed and stared out the window, watching an egret stroll down the driveway. I wanted to sit by the pool and take a nap.

Fab, hands on her hips, leaned across the island. "You're lying. You're going to spend the day feeling mopey and I'm sick of it," she yelled.

"Get over it. I'm not going." I stirred my coffee, threw the spoon in the sink, and started for the patio.

Fab grabbed my arm. "I'm calling in one of my hundreds of IOUs that say you owe me anytime I ask."

We were having our first friend fight and it was all my fault. "I don't want to go," I said quietly. "I know I haven't been that much fun, but I need a little more time."

Fab wooshed out a breath, calming slightly. "I can't do this by myself."

Didier glared at me, letting me know he'd also run out of patience, which made me feel worse; he never liked Zach. He turned Fab's face to his and said, "When do you need to leave?"

"Half an hour." Fab looked at me.

Didier turned to me, his blue eyes boring into mine. "Go get ready."

I had cracked under the tension and decided to change my mind, but I instantly changed it back with a stamp of my foot. "You can't tell me what to do!"

"Go now," he said, and pointed upstairs, "or I'll throw you over my shoulder and put your lovely ass in the shower and watch until you finish."

Fab's smirk told me I'd never win this argument. We stared at one another. I thought about my T-shirt, all wet, sticking to my body.

"Okay." Didier pushed back his stool.

I shrieked and ran upstairs, yelling, "I hate you both."

* * *

It felt good to put on my work outfit, grabbing up a jean skirt with plenty of pockets and a T-shirt, my Glock in its holster at the small of my back. Since I had no patience to tame my wild hair, I opted for a ponytail.

Coming down the stairs, I noticed the silence and quietly poked my head in the kitchen. Fab stared back, sitting at the island.

"Didier left," she said, and laughed. "He had a photo shoot in Miami."

"I'm sorry. I just wanted to stay home and be mopey, as you put it."

"Those days are over." Fab shook her finger. "Just so you know, if Didier hadn't intervened, I planned to drag you out of here by your hair."

"It was my lucky day when you broke into my house. Now take me to the café so I can get a caramel, whipped cream ton-of-calories coffee."

Fab held out the car keys. "Would you like to drive?"

"Hell no," I said, and laughed. "We don't have all day—as you constantly remind me."

* * *

Fab rocketed down the Overseas Highway past tidal flats and teal waters dotted by distant islands. The two-lane highway in each direction stretched across expanses of water, the Atlantic spreading out to the left and the Gulf to the right.

"How's life with Didier?" I asked.

"He's the only man I've ever been with I don't have to hide who I am. We discuss my cases. He talks me out of the ones where I'd be jumping out of second-floor windows—thank goodness I landed in the trash that time—and the cases where guns would be a sure thing. He jerks me back from my reckless plans and plants my feet solidly back on firm ground. His most effective method is those baby blues of his turned on me as he says softly, 'You disappoint me, love.' I'd rather fight."

"Would he have followed through on his threat this morning?" My cheeks glowed pink with embarrassment.

"He worries about you." She looked at me. "I asked him the same thing and he just laughed." Fab cut around another SUV and back in front. "Probably."

I thought about calling his bluff, but was grateful

I'd lost my nerve. "What's this case about and why do you have a bookie for a client?"

"Doug Scott, a.k.a. 'The Client.' He's a referral from Brick. It's a dispute with one of his clients over money and who owed what. The Swan brothers boosted his Mercedes and decided to hold the car hostage until the debt was settled, so Doug paid up, but then they refused to return the car. Doug, having bought the car from Brick, had him activate the locator box and we know its location."

"A Brick job?"

Fab had her own private investigator license and took jobs from him that required her "special" investigation skills. She could pick a lock in seconds, and with no fear of heights, she had no trouble scaling the sides of buildings.

Zach always called her on his hard-core jobs; that's how she and I met. Zach regretted ever introducing us. We became fast friends and I jumped at the chance to be her back-up, running interference in most cases.

"This is a simple job. We drive up, I've got a key. I'll get behind the wheel and we both drive away. No shots exchanged, hopefully." Fab turned onto Duval Street and, to her credit, her driving had been less hair-raising than usual. Today, she slowed for bikers and walkers.

"Last time we had a job in Key West, I saved your life," I reminded her. That had been yet another retrieval job that seemed so simple; that is, until a homeless drug addict appeared out of nowhere with his paws on Fab and his eyes on her ride.

Key West is one of my favorite vacation spots, with a combo of sun, water, and friendly people, not to mention my faves—shopping and food. I'd taken every tour, learning the highlights of the southernmost tip of the United States. Hemingway's house was a standout; I loved the six-toed cats that were in residence.

After a few turns, Fab pointed to the white Mercedes sitting in front of a wood one-story conch-style house, typical on this particular block.

"There it is," she said.

The tangerine-colored residence sat on low posts, and although a front porch ran the width of the house, there was not a single chair.

I unhooked my seatbelt and twisted around in the seat, looking up and down the street. "Based on our track record, this is too easy. Take your time and circle the block."

"Doesn't look like anyone is home." Fab drove slowly, checking out the neighbors on each side.

I sat on my knees and hung on to the back of the seat. A nineties black Chevy Impala caught my eye, the windows down. Someone on the passenger side ducked and crouched down out of view.

"Since I don't believe in coincidence, I think we've got company," I said. "Any reason someone else would like to hook up with the Swan brothers?"

"Word on the street is that the brothers are a pair to stay away from. I'll park around the corner, sneak back, and poke a gun in the window to get some answers."

"That's a terrible idea. Park and I'll walk by the car and casually check it out like I live in the neighborhood."

I swept my hair into a ponytail and fished out my largest pair of dark sunglasses from the console. It took

49

less than five minutes to circle the block on foot and arrive back at the SUV.

"Tell me why the DEA is staking out that house?" I hopped back into my SUV. To my shock, I knew the man crouched in the front seat. We watched a dark-haired guy round the corner from the opposite direction, grocery bag in his arms. He sauntered slowly, checking out every house before climbing into the driver's side of the sedan.

"What are you talking about?" Fab groaned.

"Paulo, your regrettable one-night stand, is staked out in the car with a bag of Cheetos and a soda. I'm guessing his partner, Grove, just joined him with another bag of junk food." Paulo and Grove were a grungy pair of undercover detectives, and friends of Brick's brother, Casio, a Miami police detective who I heard got another promotion. "I suppose Paulo also whispered drunken French to you?"

"Italian." Fab looked at me and we laughed. "I can't deal with him. He's a pig."

"I hope they remember me when I climb in the backseat, and don't shoot me." I jerked my beach bag over the seat and shimmied out of my jean skirt. I wrapped a cotton sarong around my middle, put on a tankini top, tied my T-shirt around my waist to hide my Glock, and slid back into my flip-flops.

"I'm hoping if I appeal to them on a slutty level they'll find me amusing."

Fab watched open-mouthed. "I love that you're back."

"If I'm not back in five, I don't know what." I got out of the SUV. "How do I look?"

"Trashy, sexy." Fab twisted her finger and I

turned around. "It looks like you don't have any underwear on."

I rolled my eyes, mumbling, "Just great."

I meandered up to the Impala, my eyes focused on the Mercedes and the house where it sat parked. Paulo and Grove hunched down in the seat eating chips, orangey dust on their cheeks. I leaned in the window.

"Hi, guys. Remember me?"

"Nice rack." Grove wiped his mouth with his hand and rubbed chip dust on his pants. "Sorry, girlie, we're not into hookers, and besides, it's illegal." He shook his finger.

"You need to leave," Paulo barked. "Now."

"That's not very friendly, Paulo," I said, helping myself to a chip. "We're here to retrieve the Mercedes over there and it would be nice not to get shot at or arrested."

"We?" They both said in unison and looked around.

"You remember the delicious Fabiana, don't you?" I eyed Paulo. He needed a shower and so did his partner. Neither appeared capable of the jungle sex that Fab enjoyed.

"That delectable French chick hates him," Grove snickered. "You could introduce me."

I didn't bother to tell them she'd said something with the word 'pig' in it. "Mind if I sit in the back? I'll call Casio, ask him to ask you real nice-like to do us a favor?"

"I remember now. You killed the drug dealer."

"No, I shot the drug dealer. He died in police custody a few days later, not from the gunshot, but

Deborah Brown

because he tried to escape out the window and fell to his death," I reminded them.

"We got a conflict. We want the car, so get lost," Paulo said.

Grove and Paulo were now staring out the front windshield. I was sure Fab was wiggling her butt up the block. She crossed in front of the car, and leaned in on Paulo's side. "We want the Mercedes. We've got the owner's permission to pick it up."

Paulo licked his lips, practically salivating. "The last thing you want to do is get in that car. The trunk is full of drugs."

"If you don't mind my asking," I said, "do the drugs belong to Doug the bookie or the Swan brothers?"

"There's a much bigger picture going on here," Grove said, and wagged his finger. "You two need to sashay your lovely asses back to your car, leave Key West, and go shop or whatever women do." He had run out of patience once he figured out he wasn't going to get lucky.

"Fabiana." Paulo flashed her a greasy smile. "Before you leave, give me your number."

Fab gave him the finger and stomped off.

Poor Paulo looked crushed. Did he think he stood a chance after their first disastrous coupling?

"Thanks, guys. If you're ever up in Tarpon Cove, stop by Jake's and tell them free drink on Madison." I waved.

I beat it up the street and jumped into the SUV. "That could've been way worse, like prison for years. Florida takes a dim view on drugs; a whole trunk-load could draw life. What are you going to tell Doug?"

"I should've known. Doug never does anything that anyone involved in doesn't get screwed. I'm telling Brick he can take care of the situation or I quit. It's his friend or whatever. The bright side is that we get paid and no shots were fired."

"You know, Paulo's kind of hot. If he had a shower, washed his hair, and had on clean clothes..." I managed to say with a straight face.

Chapter 9

We left The Bakery Café, the last of my latte clutched in my hand, Fab well into her second cup. The guy ahead of us in line told the cashier that he drank seven cups of coffee a day, and it made me jittery thinking about the hot mess I'd be after all that caffeine.

My phone vibrated on the dash. Damn! I hated when it flipped to silent all on its own. Not recognizing the number, I answered it anyway and hit speaker. "None of your business," didn't apply to Fab, and I was now in the habit of letting her listen in since it was easier and faster than repeating every word.

"This is Ann, Tucker Davis's assistant. The reading of Gus Ivers' will is tomorrow afternoon here at the office. Mr. Davis asked that I call and inform you." She had worked for Tucker since he opened his practice, and carried loyalty to a new level. I suspected she was also in love with him and still as snotty and condescending as I remembered.

Tucker had been my Aunt Elizabeth's choice of probate lawyer and a big pain in my butt; not to mention he almost got me killed because he wanted to get his greedy hands on her property. "What does that have to do with me?" Ann was about to find out that two could have a surly attitude.

"I'm sure it doesn't come as a surprise that you were mentioned in the will," she snorted. "Relay this same

54

message to your criminal friend, Miss Merceau. I don't have a number for her."

Fab gave the finger to my phone.

"I dare you to say that to Miss Merceau's face. I'd enjoy watching you get your ass kicked." I smiled at Fab.

"Elizabeth Hart didn't know you very well or she'd never have left you her estate."

"You can go—" I started, but heard the click of her phone.

Fab rolled her eyes. "Good thing your aunt's estate is settled and you don't have to deal with her anymore. Why do you suppose old man Ivers mentioned us in his will?"

"Could be the car wash. Our contract stated that I get to purchase the other half," I said. "We're certainly going to show up and find out."

Tolbert had called with a simple request to evict a brother/sister combo who had moved into Ivers' car wash. When the deal went awry, as some of them seem to do, I ended up owning half the business.

"Have Apple and Angie managed to get arrested yet?" Fab asked.

I hired two slightly reformed drunks to wash cars half naked and they rapidly became the new tourist attraction. "They manage to stay sober in the daytime and make a small profit slithering over cars covered in bubbles. They think I don't know that they took up residence in the storage room. I'm hoping they'll move before I have to be mean and kick them to the curb."

"They selling sexual favors yet?"

I shook my head. "I got an interesting complaint from a disgruntled customer, angry because first time he got his truck washed, Angie gave him a hand job. Next time he showed up, she refused him and his auto because he didn't tip."

Fab rolled her eyes. "You made that up."

"I'm not here to entertain you. Anyway, I laughed at the guy, told him he was a cheap bastard and hung up."

"What happens when they get arrested for prostitution?"

"It goes back to coin-operated." And I would put up a for sale sign.

My phone rang again. I looked at the screen and thought this can't be good. "Hi, Kevin." Kevin Cory, a local sheriff, was friendly with my brother but not the rest of the family. My guess, he hoped his sister would move on and not make the relationship permanent.

"Miss January has been arrested. Do you want to come down and bail her out here at the office or should I have her transferred to the women's jail?"

"Why? And who would arrest her?" I asked. Miss January had been a tenant at The Cottages since Elizabeth bought the place. She was a young drunk who looked double her age, riddled with cancer, and managed to stay alive on a diet of chain smoking and vodka.

"I did," he snapped. "Are you coming or not?"

"I'm on my way," I said, and he hung up. "You need to drop yourself at home. I need to make a jail run."

* * *

It didn't take long to cruise down to the docks where the sheriff's office is located. A small building with a dozen employees, they had a few jail cells and used them primarily as a holding area until the arrestee could be transported to the county jail if not released.

"What are the charges?" I demanded when Kevin stepped up to the front desk.

"Let's go outside," he said, and pointed to the door. "I'm fine, thanks for asking. You can lose your patronizing attitude; better me finding her drunk ass than Johnson."

I took a deep breath. "Thank you for not booking her into the scary girl's jail."

I'd never actually been inside the women's jail. The closest I'd gotten was video chat, which had a view of the inside of prison life; men's or women's side, they all complained about the food.

"She's hanging out with people who have felony rap sheets. Carly Martin, her newest best friend, has two pages of arrests. They stole Carly's mother's car and went joyriding and were found inside, passed out drunk down by the docks, motor running. Mrs. Martin has since recanted, mumbling something about a misunderstanding."

I thought I had gotten rid of Carly, the neighborhood drunk, by threatening bodily harm. "What happens now?"

"Miss January is free to go. But that's not the way it's going to play out." He glared at me. "She thinks she's been officially arrested. I personally put her through fingerprints, had her picture taken, and made her change into jail issued clothes. She's currently taking a snooze in a cell. I told her I contacted you to bail her out and you said you'd think about it. Then I told her if you didn't show up soon I'd put her on a jail bus, where she'd go through another booking process, strip search, and sit in a cell for a month until her trial."

"If this works, I'll make an effort to be nice to your partner." Miss January didn't used to take her drunkcapades off the property until she started making new drunk friends.

"Johnson's put in for a transfer and I hope he gets it. One more thing, I think Carly is stealing from Miss January and that's why she's always out of money. Carly drunk-mumbled something about getting money from Miss January and when I asked her about it, she didn't know anything. I will admit it's damn hard to get reliable info out of drunks."

I felt bad for Kevin. I know my attitude changed toward him because of his partner. "I'll play my part to the hilt and let her know she owes me for bailing her out."

The door opened and Miss January came shuffling out, swollen red eyes, looking scared.

"Thanks, Kevin." I walked over and put my arm around her boney shoulder. "Ready to go home, little jailbird?" I asked her.

Life had been hard on Miss January. Starting with her husband's murder, she took to alcohol to numb her grief and never looked back. Now at forty years old, she looked eighty and her days were numbered since being diagnosed with cancer, which she medicated with vodka.

"It's terrible here, they don't let you smoke or drink," she sniffed. "Carly wanted me to say I stole the car, but I didn't."

"I know you didn't, Miss J." I hugged her, opening the SUV door and helping her in. "Listen to me, no more fun and games with Carly, you got that, or I'll be quite angry with you and send my mother over to lecture your ears off. She's very good and won't let you nod off until she's finished."

"Don't you worry, missy. I'm going to behave myself."

If only I believed her.

Chapter 10

Shirl came out of the office door just as I pulled into Miss January's parking space to the side of her cottage. She had fallen asleep as soon as I buckled her seat belt.

Joseph, my other long-term tenant, had rented his space out in the past as temporary parking for stolen cars. Once the sheriff vacated the neighborhood, the car wanted for questioning would magically relocate itself. Threat of eviction put a stop to that enterprising operation.

"Can I get your help?" I called to Shirl. Renting to a nurse had its perks; she kept a watchful eye on the tenants. Recently, one of the guests from the UK cut his foot at the beach and she cleaned and bandaged it, which made her an instant favorite.

We woke Miss January and helped her inside her cottage. We put her on the bed and she went right back to sleep, snoring softly. I marveled that her cottage was spotless, nothing in the way of knick knacks. The only oddity, her dead cat that had been stuffed by an amateur, lay on the couch. We left quietly and I told Shirl what happened.

Mac joined us in the driveway. "Carly Martin doesn't set foot on this property," I said.

A red two-door pickup piled with an assortment of junk blew into the driveway, going way too fast, scraping the underside. Three people were crammed into the front seat, Kathy on the passenger side. They blocked the driveway and seven people in total piled out of the truck. Kathy got out, dressed in a bathing suit skirt, flashing cotton underwear and a button-down blouse.

"That's her husband, Ron," Mac stage-whispered when the driver's door opened and a thirty-something-year-old man got out, with boy-next-door good looks.

"At least they don't look like mother and son," I said. His wife looked older, but not by twenty years. "You triple swear you checked these two out?" I asked Mac.

"Here she comes." Shirl nudged me.

Kathy approached us with a big pile of cheap beads around her neck, looking like she just returned from a Mardi Gras celebration.

"Hello, everyone," Kathy cooed. "The store got in new necklaces." She ran her fingers through them, removing three green strands of dyed shells and handing them to us. They still had the price tag hanging off the clasps. I wondered if she expected payment, in which case I'd hand mine back.

"You're so nice to us," Shirl said. "I wore the scarf you gave me to work the other day and got so many compliments."

Something about Kathy made me suspicious; all that niceness, the sincere looking smile but hard, calculating eyes, which once again scanned the property and the street. The price tag also hung off the side of her skirt. Did she wear the clothes from her beach souvenir store and then return them? Or her idea of a quirky advertising idea? I watched the three women talk, realizing Kathy Stone had charmed my manager and tenant.

"Stop by the store sometime," Kathy said to me.

"We can get to know one another better."

"Sounds great," I said. It didn't, but "hell no" sounded unfriendly.

"Enjoy your necklaces. If you need more you know where you can find them," Kathy gushed. "Have to go! We're moving in the last of our boxes and then I'll have hungry friends to feed."

"Ask your husband to slow down in the driveway," I said to her, then added, "please."

"Ron got busy running his mouth and that lead foot of his…" She giggled.

Once Kathy was out of earshot Shirl said, "Those two have a lot of friends. Party every night, but surprisingly, they're not loud. People come and go all night long. I wonder how they get to work the next day."

I motioned them over to the barbeque area where we could sit and talk and our voices wouldn't carry down the driveway. "When are they moving?"

"Three month contract. I drove by their new house. It's under renovation; workers inside and out. Ron's construction sign is in the yard," Mac said.

"The house actually exists?" I asked.

"You always this suspicious?" Shirl played with her hair, flipping it around, and then looked down her top.

"You should have seen some of our prior renters; my personal favorite, the murderer."

"I'm telling you, I'm on it this time. Checked out the old place, the new one, and even went by her store. I got there early enough to watch her unlock the door and let two women come in who were waiting," Mac said. "Shirl is right about the constant coming and going of the cars; they tend to fill up the driveway, but since it's so late, none of the neighbors have complained and the sheriff hasn't stopped by in a long time."

"Don't forget you need a sign." Shirl nudged Mac.

"The owners of the yellow house called last night," she said, and pointed across the street, "decided to hire me as property manager. The last renters left the place a mess. I had it cleaned already and sent pictures, showing them there are no slackers over here. I need a sign temporarily. I'll use one of the cheap 'For Rent' signs until they send back the signed contract. I've spread the news, no undesirables."

A nice Canadian couple owned that house and a block-style duplex down the street, and both had seen colorful tenants in the past. A background check exposed criminals, but for drunks and addicts you had to hone your radar for the tell-tale signs. Most rental companies weren't interested in working for property owners with only one or two properties, and the last company they used ripped them off with unnecessary repair bills. The owners approached me on their last visit and I recommended Mac under the condition that she never leave me to deal with my own tenants. I told her if this worked out, I'd help her solicit other out-of-state owners with one or two properties.

"I guess you won't be renting to locals." I stood and walked to my SUV. "First sign of trouble, call me."

Chapter 11

"Couldn't you drive across someone's lawn so we can get out of this traffic and get to the reading of the will on time?" I scrunched my nose at Fab. Traffic cones had funneled two lanes into one for roadwork. "Don't you dare give me any finger sign language or I'll push you out of my SUV and make you walk."

Fab gave me a tight-lipped look. "Your phone is ringing."

"Hello, detective," I said, after I hit the speaker. "Let me guess, you want me to come to your office so you can arrest me?" I enjoyed sparring with Harder, being friends had its perks. I liked him, and, more importantly, trusted him. He looked for the truth, not the most expedient way to close his files.

"Smart ass. Time for you to step up and do me a favor. Find out when Ivers' will and testament will be read?"

"Favor means you would owe me." I pictured him clenching his jaw. "Why would I know anything about the Ivers estate?"

"Creole says you know or can find out. Is he full of it or not?" Harder demanded.

I almost squealed as Fab knocked over a cone, jumped the curb, and cut around the back of a pawn shop. "Me and your favorite criminal are on our way to the reading now."

Fab slugged me on the shoulder.

"Ow!" I pointed to the street for her to pay attention.

"Do you have me on speaker?" He sounded irritated. "Now I owe Creole five bucks; I bet him you only did that sneaky ass trick on him. Heads up, though, Creole's not happy with you."

I sighed. "What now?"

"Not long after you and your friend left Key West without the Mercedes, a gunfight broke out. The Swan brothers screwed another dealer and bullets flew when they went to retrieve their illegal product. Happy ending, they're all in jail, three of them are still in the hospital, but the downside is that it looks like they'll live."

"Fab and I were there to pick up the lawfully-registered owner's car." I shook my head at Fab. "Why us?" I mouthed.

"Where is Doug?" Harder asked. "He's nowhere to be found and we'd like to have a friendly sit down with him."

"We don't know and don't care. Doug will never be a client in the future." I changed the subject, asking, "Why not call your pal, Tucker Davis, about Ivers' will?"

"Tucker took exception to the fact I didn't like being screwed on one of his business deals. I obviously can't make the reading. Listen up; I want to know who's there. Who's acting weird? If you're going you must be mentioned in the will, so ask for a copy, you're entitled."

Fab rounded the corner fast, making me rock in my seat. She had stuck to the back streets, getting ahead of construction, having to U-turn and double back a few blocks, but at least we'd almost be on time.

65

"And I get what?" I asked.

"Satisfaction for doing something nice," Harder said, and chuckled.

"That's not enough. Does this have anything to do with Ivers' autopsy?"

"You know I can't discuss an open case. Get me what I want and I'll be nice to you sometime." Harder hung up.

"You do realize he said open case? That means Ivers' death might not have been natural," Fab said.

* * *

Tucker Davis, scurvy attorney-at-law, had taken an old cottage-style house—a corner lot located just after you breezed past the welcome-to-town sign—and turned it into office space. The outside had been the recipient of a fresh coat of yellow paint. Personally, I liked the previous blue color. My favorite addition was the old wooden rowboat that held his sign. I'd like to stage an intervention for the boat and drag it home and display it in my front yard, junking the sign.

Fab pulled into the small parking lot, and, unable to maneuver the SUV into the last space, parked on the lawn. She caught me rolling my eyes.

"Try and behave yourself," Fab said, as she shook her finger at me.

"We'll see who pulls their gun first." I smirked.

The front door chimed when opened. That was new and it made me wonder if someone had snuck in besides me. The ultra-modern interior didn't fit the charm of the outside. Out of the corner of my eye, I caught a glimpse of Ann standing at the reception desk so I helped myself to a fistful of candy from the coffee table. Arms across her chest and a scowl on her face, she glared as I dropped my loot into my purse. "You're late," she said. She tapped her watch as her dark eyes bore into us.

"Two minutes is not late," Fab told her, baring her teeth.

Ann wouldn't mess with Fab since her reputation as an unstable wild card preceded her; most people didn't know the hype was exaggerated, unless provoked. She stepped back and opened the door and we both had to squeeze by her as she blocked most of the opening, having packed a few pounds on her middle-aged frame.

"Follow me and try not to interrupt when you go into Mr. Davis's office," she snarled.

Besides Tucker, seven people were crammed into his office. His desk took up three-quarters of the space, which left a tiny, uncomfortable area for the rest of us. Fab spotted Tolbert and slid into the chair next to him. Feeling claustrophobic, I stood by the window, leaning against the low sill. I recognized Violet Ivers and if I hadn't seen a picture, I'd have guessed her to be Gus's daughter by her big, howling sobs. Three other men whom I didn't recognize filled the chairs. Tucker acknowledged me with his hard, cold brown eyes.

Why in the world did the old people in Tarpon Cove choose a weasel like Tucker to draw up their wills when he built his practice on criminal law by getting guilty defendants off? His court record was near perfect, he rarely lost a case. Juries bonded with him despite the fact that his clients were low-life scum. The joke around town was that if you had Tucker for a criminal lawyer, you did it and have the money for his exorbitant fees.

I leaned across to the candy bowl sitting on Tucker's desk and helped myself to another handful, knowing it would irritate him. I threw it in my purse, joining the other candy to be eaten on the way home. He didn't say a word, but glared and moved the bowl to the cabinet behind his desk. Aging had been unkind to him, his brown hair turning gray in odd clumps and turning his complexion sallow. One thing he had in common with his assistant, Ann, they both looked like they had something permanently stuck in an unpleasant place.

Tucker pulled a thick file of paperwork out of a side drawer and announced to everyone that as executor he'd be handling the distribution of the Ivers estate according to the deceased's wishes. He cleared his throat and started reading, boring everyone to tears with legalese. I wanted to yell, "Hurry up, already!"

Violet had calmed somewhat and squirmed around in her chair, hiccupping. One would guess her to be a middle-aged woman, but she was dressed like a six-year-old in a full dress that tied in a bow behind her back, completing the look with Mary Jane shoes and loose blonde curls.

"I have an envelope here for each one of you from Gus," Tucker said, acknowledging us individually as he held them up flopping them back and forth. "But I'll be keeping these in my control until the estate is finalized." He tossed them onto the corner of his desk.

"Tolbert, Ivers left you that parcel of land that joins your properties at the back and a check for that so-called church of yours." Tucker eyed him in a disrespectful way.

Fab glared at Tucker; I thought she'd pistol whip him. He noticed and glared back at her. "You got a problem with me, girlie, you can leave, and I'll mail you a copy of the will."

I spoke up. "Fab's staying. She's my ride home." I gave Tucker my best I-dare-you- face, letting him know I'd make a scene in his office and not care who witnessed.

"Charlie, Bob, and John, Ivers left you sizeable bequests." Tucker stopped to take a drink of water. He passed each man a piece of paper, presumably with an amount written down as they all smiled and nodded, pleased with what they saw.

John, apparently an Ivers, made me wonder where he fit in the family gene pool. The familial connection surprised me since neither he nor Violet looked at the other. Interesting, too, that Tucker knew everyone in the room; they must be locals after all.

Ann walked in with a tray of cold drinks, serving the others, and ignoring Fab and I.

Fab spoke up. "Annie, I'll take a bottle of water. Madison wants one, too."

I tried not to laugh and shook my head in agreement.

"I'm not sure why, Miss Merceau," Tucker said, glancing her way, "but Gus left you his antique gun collection. I would hope it's not because you coerced him in anyway, but one never knows how low you'd draw the line."

Tucker wiped the look of joy off Fab's face with his ugly insinuations. She jumped up and I jerked on the back of her shirt, holding tight until she sat back down. Tolbert laced his fingers in hers and squeezed. I flipped

Tucker the finger, mouthing the words at the same time.

His eyes snapped with anger, clenching his hand into a fist. "Miss Westin, I realize you were part owners with Gus in the car wash but for whatever reason he left you the rest of the block."

I cut him off. "If you think this is the best time to fling dirt, I'm happy to play."

"I wouldn't put it past you to pressure an old man in an unseemly way." Tucker smiled.

To hell with being embarrassed. "Like you did to my aunt? It mystifies me why you are not in jail."

Everyone sat stunned, mostly looking down at their feet—except Violet, who glared openly.

Gus and I had a business relationship, but I never expected anything from him and, quite frankly, not even the other half of Clean Bubbles. We had a signed agreement, but never finalized all of the details because he continually dragged his feet, calling for meetings where we ended up talking for a couple of hours and he'd flirt outrageously with Fab.

Tucker shuffled through more papers, making a few notes before looking up. "The rest of the estate goes to Violet Ivers. We'll discuss everything when everyone has left." He smiled at her.

"Who are those two?" Violet shrieked, pointing at me and Fab. "Why would Daddy leave them spit?" Her voice high pitched and whiney like that of a spoiled child. She'd been sitting demurely, hands in her lap, her pasty face splotched red from her hysterics.

Tucker patted her hand, passing the tissue box, and then broke the awkward silence. "I wondered the same thing. Don't you worry, my dear Violet. I'll do a thorough investigation before the estate is settled."

"You don't think they influenced Daddy in an unseemly way, do you?" Violet raked her eyes over Fab.

Fab leaned forward. "Mind your manners, bitch. I bite."

Violet hissed and jerked back. "You're uncouth." Apparently her childish tone was permanent. "I don't want her grubby hands on anything Daddy worked his life for; that's not right."

Tolbert pulled Fab back into her chair and put his arm around her shoulder. Fab unleashed a tirade in French.

The men, hoping for a roll-on-the-floor girl fight, had their eyes glued to the two women. I momentarily thought about brandishing my Glock and shooting into the ceiling, but knew Tucker would have me arrested.

Tucker cleared his throat. "You know, Miss Westin and Merceau, this is the kind of disruptive crap I expect from your ilk. If I weren't bound by propriety, you would've never been allowed to set foot in my office." He took a breath. "This meeting is over. All of you will get a copy of the will once I've opened probate. My advice is not to foolishly spend money you don't have, as I'm advising my client, Miss Ivers, to contest."

"When and where is the memorial service?" I asked Violet, trying to hide my loathing.

Her hands clenched. "You're certainly not invited; in fact, none of you are." She covered her face and burst into tears.

Tolbert gasped at Violet's words in shock. "But, Violet. I'd like to have a memorial service."

"I said no," she sobbed. "You're not invited,

71

either."

The sadness that rolled across Tolbert's face squeezed my heart. I just wanted to console him...after dragging Violet from her chair by her hair and slapping her senseless.

Fab jumped up and every man watched her wiggle her way out of the office in her tight black skirt, five-inch heels, and chest-hugging pullover top. "Hey, Annie, where's our water?" she yelled in the hallway.

Chapter 12

Strong hands caressed my body. Nimble fingers trailed along my sides, tracing patterns along my arms before sliding up my cheek and softly around my lips. I stirred, and stretched like a lazy cat, smiling, not wanting to leave the warmth of the dream. My eyes opened slowly, taking several seconds to adjust to the predawn light filtering in through my windows. I see the figure lying next to my body and jump, but before I could scream, a hand clamped over my mouth.

"Shh, it's me," Creole whispered in my ear, nibbling on the lobe. A sliver of light from the full moon shined across his face through the window.

I hissed, "You've got a lot of damned nerve! This is my bedroom, get out."

"No, I'm being a gentleman." He kissed the corner of my mouth. "Besides, I came by to check on you." He wrapped his hands in my shirt and lifted me off the pillow, giving me a slight shake. "I heard about Key West. Where was your Glock?"

"We were back on the Overseas Highway before the bullets flew." I was extremely grateful Fab and I didn't end up in the middle of a drug war. Creole's lips were now a tight hard line. "I had it holstered to the small of my back. And if it gives you peace of mind, I'm not leaving it at home anymore."

He pushed me back against the pillows, pulling

the sheet down a little. "Whose is this?" He fingered the white men's dress shirt I slept in these days. He threw one of his long legs across my lower body in case I thought about taking flight.

"Mine." I had donated all old shirts once worn by the ex-boyfriend.

"When are you starting range practice again?" He pulled me hard against his side so that my head rested on his shoulder.

"I booked time with my instructor for next week."

He wrapped his fingers in my hair, pulling my face up to look at him. He pressed his mouth over mine. "I just worry about you," he said against my lips.

It felt so good to be trapped like this, powerlessly and breathlessly waiting for his next move. I didn't have to wait long. His mouth slammed against mine, and his tongue slid into my mouth. He tasted so good. I surrendered willingly.

When he broke the kiss, I moaned. His head tipped, and then moved down again. "I want you," he growled in my ear. He pulled me back across him and I turned to face him, my head in the middle of his chest. "But not like this. Our first time is not going to be ambush sex."

I looked up at him. "You've given this forgone conclusion some thought, have you?" One more kiss and I could be naked in a hot second.

He held my face in his hand. "I want a real date. During-dinner foreplay," he said, and bit my lip. "Something intimate, for two, and then I'll fuck you breathless." He kissed me again. "It's going to take hours, not some stupid quickie, although I wouldn't be adverse to that in the future."

I struggled to breathe.

He rolled me over and on to my side, wrapping his arms around me and drawing me into the protective curve of his shoulder. I ran all the what-ifs through my mind and how it might affect our family if we got together only to break up.

"Shh." He patted my head. "You're thinking too much." He hooked his leg across my hip, pulling me closer, if that was possible.

After a while I snuggled against him and fell back asleep.

* * *

"I have to leave," Creole whispered and pulled me to the end of bed. He buried his hand in the hair at the back of my neck, rolling me over, kissing me. Softly at first, his tongue skimmed my lips, forcing them open for a ruthless kiss.

One more, this time gently, he put his lips to mine before leaving the bedroom, my mouth still tingling from his previous kiss. I looked at myself reflected in the mirror, lips reddened and swollen, face flushed, and my hair a wild mess.

I whispered at the top of the stairs, "What are we going to say?"

He looked amused. "About what?" He half dragged me into the kitchen, enjoying my discomfort.

Both Fab and Didier stared as we entered the room; they didn't hide their shocked looks. We exchanged good mornings and lapsed into an awkward silence. Why was I the only one to look as if I had enjoyed a night of mind-numbing sex? They'd never believe that we had only slept together—I almost didn't.

Didier recovered first. "If you like it strong, coffee is ready," he said to Creole, pointing to the fresh pot.

I grabbed mugs from the cupboard. "Don't forget, barbeque here later." I looked at Fab. "Are you weaseling out?"

"We'll be there," Didier answered for her.

Fab glared at me and had me wondering who she was madder at Creole, for sneaking in past her radar, or me, since she didn't have the details of last night yet. I liked Creole a lot, now all I needed to do was swallow my fear and agree to a "first date."

Creole put his arm across my chest, holding me close while he laughed with Didier. One might wonder what a male model and drug enforcement agent had in common, and as it turns out, they both bike to stay in shape. Creole told him about a private beach he'd take him to where they could ride on the sand.

"I have to leave." Creole wiggled his finger. He took my mug and his and put them in the sink.

I blushed deep red, afraid to close the few steps between us, but my feet had a mind of their own. Please don't make a scene, I pleaded with my eyes. When I got close enough, his hand snaked out and jerked me into his arms. "Don't forget your Glock." He seared my lips with a thorough kiss and squeezed both butt cheeks so hard I squeaked.

To my credit, my knees didn't cave. I stood at the kitchen window watching him leave. Before getting in his truck, he waved.

"What the hell just happened?" Fab yelled.

Didier smiled his approval at me.

I covered my face. "It's not what you think." I laughed, sounding a little unhinged, and ran past them upstairs to my bedroom to relive every moment.

Chapter 13

My brother, Brad Westin, had docked his boat; he's one of the hardest working commercial fishermen, which meant fresh catch for the barbeque today. I whined his ear off on the phone about Mother fixing me up and my yelling and having a public episode.

"Damn, I miss all the good stuff," he said. "She'd stop if you'd get a boyfriend."

"I should go rent a guy who's a total skeeve and scare the heck out of her. Tell her I'm pregnant and expecting a little skeeve."

"How about we dish up some payback?" Brad's voice was full of excitement. "I'm going to tell her to leave Spoon with the babysitter, that it's just the three of us." Spoon was twelve years younger than Mother, but her genes had been kind so they looked similar in age. Brad and I expressed relief that he wasn't younger than us. He outlined his idea to ambush Mother with a fix-up.

"Who are you going to get at the last minute?" I asked.

"I've been planning this for a while. I played poker with our CPA and some of his cronies, thinking I could fleece them, and barely walked away with money for a soda. I ran the scheme past the boys and Doc Rivers jumped to be bait, saying it sounded like fun. I'll call him."

Brad's plans surprised me. Mother hadn't

meddled in his life since he hooked up with Julie, but she drove him crazy before, like she's doing to me now. I liked Doc Rivers, a retired doctor who made house calls and was friend to both my late Aunt Elizabeth and Zach. "Doc is perfect as long as he knows it's a fake setup. What about when Spoon finds out?"

"What's he going to do?" Brad's laugh was evil. "I called the cook at Jake's and gave him a list of what we'd need for dinner, all you need to do is pick it up. Julie is bringing the dessert after Liam decides which one."

* * *

I loved long showers. Forcing myself to get out, I managed to pull myself together for the family barbeque. My eyes sparkled; one would have to be crazy not to enjoy Creole's all-consuming kisses. I threw my new bathing suit and black and white sheer wrap skirt that hung mid-calf onto the bed. I would change when I got back from Jake's. Until then, I pulled on a short black full skirt and a short-sleeve top. A skirt was always my first choice in clothing; I wore pants only when I went somewhere cold, which I tried to avoid.

I snuck out the front door without running into Fab. At some point I'd have to answer to her intense questioning. She'd interrogate me like a cop, although I'm pretty sure she wouldn't point a gun. She needed to learn patience since our chat would have to wait until later when there was no chance of anyone eavesdropping. By then, I'd think of something to say.

* * *

The driveway to Jake's had been blocked by sheriff's cars with blinking lights. I groaned. "Who died now?" I had to circle the block and park on the street.

Officer Johnson jerked a young woman with dirty blonde hair across the driveway by a pair of metal cuffs. I wondered if he was responsible for the dried blood under her nose and scratches on her cheek. Head down, she yelled something incoherent. He looked annoyed at her attempt to twist away, and, opening the back of his car, he shoved her none-too-gently onto the back seat.

Kevin barely had control of a brunette who kicked at him every chance she got. "You bitch," she screeched at the top of her lungs. Apparently, this was directed at the other woman under arrest. The brunette tried to wrench free from Kevin and managed to fall onto the ground, skinning her knees. She unleashed an F-word-laced tirade on him that would make a sailor blush.

I hustled into the bar, not wanting to catch the attention of the busy sheriffs. Somehow this would all end up being my fault. The television over the bar blasted a golf game that not one person had their eyes on, and music blared from the juke box. I played golf in high school, but my best friend and I sent more chunks of grass flying than balls.

"What the hell happened?" I asked Phil, who handed me a bottle of water.

She had an ear-to-ear smile and swung her long blonde hair. "Once word gets around we had a bar fight, we'll be packed again. We need to make a 'this happened here' sign and auction the seats." A couple of her middle-aged male groupies who took up residence at the bar during her shifts laughed.

She went on. "Group of girls showed up, celebrating a birthday. After a couple of rounds, it comes out two of them are sleeping with the same guy. I passed by the juke box when the blonde blurted, 'It's bad enough I have to share him with his wife.'" Phil could multi-task, washing glasses and talking at the same time.

"The brunette finally realized her boyfriend was the man in question and said, 'He's divorced.' She lost it when the blonde mentioned he added a new hoochie to the group. That's when she jumped across the table, threw a glass of beer in her face, called her a whore, and dragged her to the floor." Phil refreshed drinks, holding court at the bar.

I shook my head. "Did you try and stop the fight?"

Phil arched her brows. "Hell no, and get a chunk of hair pulled out like the one girl? I stayed out of it. Why ruin everyone's fun? They tipped the table over, chick fight on, kicking, screaming, hair pulling, and slapping— no real punches. One of the customers called 911."

I groaned when Johnson slithered through the front door, headed in my direction. "You're a trouble magnet. If it's not The Cottages filled with felons, then it's your bar. A couple of more incidents here and I'm sure we can get this place shut down."

"Is there anything specific that you want, because I'm on my way out?" I reminded myself that I promised to try to be nicer, and failed.

"If I think of something, I'll call you."

I walked in the direction of the kitchen, turned, and yelled, "Why don't you go arrest the husband who

81

started all of this?"

Chapter 14

"Help me," I yelled, kicking open the front door, two grocery bags in my hands. Liam came running from the kitchen. "There's more food in the SUV."

Brad reached for the bags and I followed him into the kitchen. My brother was six foot tall, muscled, and tan from hard work on the open water, not a speck of red hair, his brownish hair washed out from the sun. Family lore has it my hair color came from my grandmother, whom I'd never met.

Didier leaned against the counter, giving me an assessing stare which made me blush.

"Where's Mother?" I asked, turning to hug Julie who had come to help. Mother and I liked her. Based on his past, we started to think the only women Brad could attract were ones with mental health issues.

"On her way over. She's not happy to leave Spoon home alone," Brad said, grabbing a beer from the refrigerator.

"You better hope Spoon has a sense of humor," I said. "He might get really mad."

"What's he going to do, kill me?" Brad snickered. He had taken over the kitchen, which suited all the non-cookers.

"That would probably end their sweaty sex," I said with a straight face.

"Aaah! Out of my kitchen," he said, and pointed.

Didier cornered me in the living room and slipped his arm around my shoulder. "Your new boyfriend coming today?" he whispered.

"He's not…Creole was invited." I blushed and tried to step away, but he held on to my arm.

"You look lovely as always, but you need to change into that new bathing suit of yours." He smiled.

I knew he picked out Fab's clothes and she looked hot. She tried to resist his bossy ways until one night they got into a fight over a 'stupid dress' as she called it; she got her way and felt terrible the rest of the evening. "I'm not your girlfriend."

He turned me around. "Go!" He smacked me lightly on the butt.

I wondered as I ran upstairs if his magical powers could be extended to include Mother. Now that would be a match of wills. I lay stretched out daydreaming across my bed, my eyes closed, a stupid smile on my face, when someone knocked on the door. Mother poked her head in. I jumped up and ran to hug her, pulling her onto the bed to sit next to me.

"You know you could've given Brian a chance, he's a nice young man," Mother said.

"A nice young man is the best you can do? When have I ever been attracted to anyone but a bad ass?" I asked. "What about Spoon? He doesn't fit that 'nice' category."

"He's a good man. He pursued me, plying me with whiskey and cigars and the next thing I knew…" She giggled.

"How did your conversation with Creole go?"

"He let me know that he's interested in my

daughter and not happy with my interference. Madison," she said, cupping my chin, "you and Creole getting together is a bad idea. I told him if you were really interested you would have said yes already."

I groaned. "What did he say?"

"He wasn't happy and snapped back saying that you are interested. Then he wrestled a couple of promises from me not to meddle and took me to lunch. Your name wasn't mentioned once and he kissed me when he left and said, 'Knock it off.'

"You're on the rebound," she continued. "You two get together and after a few rounds of sex and break-up, he won't want to be part of the family anymore. He's been a great addition and I want it to stay that way; he's like having a part of my sister. You two will be a lot happier with other people, and when you break up it won't impact our family. Tell him no and be done with it."

Her words shocked me. I no longer had to wonder why she opposed the two of us getting together. She made it sound like I had a track record of casual romances, which I didn't. She did have a good point, though. If we dated and it didn't work out, would Creole disappear from our lives? I want a relationship with someone who doesn't see me as a fixer, and he's never complained once about my more adventurous activities, except to tell me not to get hurt. Zach had a long list of changes he wanted me to make that eventually would have given our relationship zero chance to work.

"What did Spoon have to say about your match making?" Feeling sad, I turned my back and stared out the window, the sun shining on my face.

"Told me my fix-up skills sucked. That hurt my

feelings," Mother sniffed. "More promises about not doing it again."

I turned to her and she stared as though trying to read my mind. Knowing her and Spoon, they hadn't reached the part in their relationship where they'd had a serious disagreement.

"Word of warning, Mother: If Spoon tells you not to do something and you do it anyway, beware. He doesn't strike me as the type to put up with those girly games; he might walk out on you and you'd miss your cigar-sharing, Jack-drinking partner."

Mother seemed to mull that over. "When did you get so smart?"

"Look around, how many alpha males do we have in this family, including Didier?"

She blushed. "Didier cornered me, lifted my chin to meet his angry, ice-cold blue eyes, and he said, 'That wasn't nice what you did to Madison. It made her cry.' He glared right through me, and without a word, he walked away. I wanted to yell, 'It was only dinner,' but didn't have the nerve."

"Mother, Didier keeps a watchful eye on the three of us, in case you haven't noticed. He cares about us and our happiness. Even Julie blushes and giggles at everything he says. He doesn't take no for an answer."

"Brad is the only person not mad at me. He let me bend his sympathetic ear, we talked, and in the end he had me laughing. I like that Brad is around more, taking shorter fishing trips. One more thing about Creole: I've noticed the way he looks at you, and you're not doing anything to discourage him."

"I'll talk to him, but Creole has a mind of his

own," I said. He would not be easy to discourage since I didn't really want to, but I also didn't feel like putting a wedge between me and Mother, especially if everything went badly and it couldn't be fixed.

"You need to try harder. You just got out of a relationship; meet new people. I'd like to see you both happy with other people." Mother brushed back my hair, eyed my sweats. "You need to put something else on and get downstairs."

It shocked me how adamant Mother was about Creole and me not having a relationship.

Fab stuck her head in the door. "Ready yet?"

"Don't you knock?" I narrowed my eyes.

"Creole in here?" She looked around and laughed. "It made me happy to see you a disheveled mess this morning. I hope we see that every morning. Didier and I like him. We could actually do a couple's-something, unlike with the last guy, who disliked both me and Didier."

"What if it doesn't work out and he doesn't want to part of the family anymore?"

"He's not that big of a jerk. It doesn't have to be marriage or nothing. You may end up better friends than the two of you are already."

Chapter 15

I surveyed the living room from the top of the stairs, in a black two-piece tankini, a sheer cover-up sitting low on my hips. Locking eyes with Didier, he gave me a thumbs up. His arm hooked around Fab, who was in a skimpy bikini with a plunging neckline, and a knee-length cover up. Half way down the stairs the doorbell rang.

Julie opened it to find Doc Rivers, a tall man with a slender build and an amazing amount of white hair. He still made occasional rounds at The Cove's hospital for special patients and could be counted on for emergency house calls. Brad closed in on the two and they talked quietly. My guess was they were going over their ambush plan.

Brad introduced Doc around, saving Mother until last. "So much more appropriate for you than the criminal, don't you think?"

His comment took her by surprise, but before she could answer, Doc swooped in and pulled her into an overly long hug, running his hand down her back. "I've been looking forward to meeting you, after all the great things Brad has told me and, of course, I've known your daughter for a long time."

I watched Mother struggle with her impeccable manners, the ones she insisted that Brad and I cultivate. I felt sorry for her and decided to rescue her. Brad reading the look on my face, glared at me to stay put. In that moment, I realized his plans were far more devious than a fix-up; he'd made no secret of the fact he found Spoon to be unsuitable, a "nice guy, but go date someone else's mother."

Julie and Brad made the perfect hosts. She quietly pushed everyone outside by the pool to where she'd set up an entire table of party food to fill up on before the main course. She refilled drinks and directed people to help themselves. I hoped that Brad would soon make her my legal sister-in-law. Another perk would be my first nephew, Liam.

"When do I get to go on a job with you and Fab?" Liam asked.

We both stood at the food table. I loved nibbly food and had to work hard to restrain myself not to ruin dinner. Since we were partying at my house, I claimed the leftovers and would feast on them for days.

"Have you run this fun idea by your mother?" *Or Brad for that matter?* Liam had hinted several times about doing a ride-a-long. I thought about taking him on something totally boring but I knew from hands-on experience that some of our best ideas go horribly wrong and guns show up like a big party crasher.

"She'll probably say no. Mom flipped over the shooting at the bar." He looked unhappy.

"I didn't shoot the guy," I said. "Let me see if I can arrange a guest visit at Miami P.D." *What could go wrong?* After all, it had the criminals locked up.

"You're the best."

"I'll see if you can bring a friend, so you're not stuck with your pretend aunt all day."

Liam laughed. "You're my Auntie Homegirl."

I moved to the pool, sticking my feet in the water and watched everyone laugh and interact, feeling like a wallflower. Creole slid through the fence from the "secret" path that ran between mine and the neighbor's house. All my friends used that entrance and then walked into the house through the French doors.

He scanned the patio, looking tired and sporting facial hair. His blue eyes found what he'd been searching for, and he gave me a smirky smile. I stepped out of the pool as he closed the space between us. He pulled me into a hug, murmuring, "Twice in one day."

I could barely stop myself from pushing into him.

Brad called to Creole from the barbeque, "Come meet Mother's date. You know everyone else." He had replaced Elizabeth's old kettle cooker with a super-duper model. It didn't bother me that I didn't even know how to turn it on.

Mother's eyes snapped with anger, first at Brad and then me.

Doc Rivers flicked his fingers through Mother's hair and patted her on the head. She stiffened but didn't move away.

Creole linked his arm through mine. "I hope she's enjoying herself." He looked at me. "Oh no you don't, do not feel sorry for her or she'll be fixing you up again."

"Hey, Doc," Creole said, and extended his hand.

They greeted one another as old friends. That made sense to me sort of, since Zach and Doc had been good friends and Doc knew Zach's family. Creole and Zach had grown up as childhood friends, only to go their separate ways as adults.

Creole maneuvered my body in front of his, one

arm across my chest. He brushed my hair back over my shoulder, nibbling my neck and then biting down. My body jumped, he held me tight and I bit my lip to keep from yelling, "Ouch."

He ran his finger over my neck. "My teeth marks look good."

I caught Mother's frown, not happy over Creole's attention, or that I hadn't done one thing to discourage him. All eyes turned to watch, probably wondering if he'd strip off my clothes. This was the first time he'd made his feelings known in such a public way. Fab and Didier whispered and then both openly smirked. Didier and Creole had the friendly guy thing going on. That ease of male bonding had never been achieved with Zach.

"I left a package in your bedroom. Don't open it until you're ready to go to sleep." He had his other hand now squarely on my butt cheek squeezing in a pleasant way.

I grabbed his hand and pulled him over to the other side of the pool, away from everyone. We ignored the death stare from Fab, effectively blocking any of her eavesdropping attempts.

I came to an abrupt halt and put my hand on his chest. "We can't get involved." His blue eyes stared intently. "You're part of the family now, we can't mess that up for sex. We break up and then everything gets awkward."

He sunk his fingers into my cheeks. "I don't know what goes on in that head of yours, but we are going to happen so get used to it. And we're not breaking up."

"What if we have sex and it's terrible? The last one complained I used him for sex and sometimes I did.

91

Or I break your heart and you divorce the family?"

His mouth curved at the corners. "You've been talking to your mother; her promises lasted about five minutes. What other ridiculous questions do you have?"

"Mother made her point patently clear—she doesn't want us to get together. I'm not interested in having my family mad at me."

"I find it very insulting that the only thing you might find enjoyable is my…sex, and not for that long."

Brad yelled out, "Dinner's ready."

"You need to think about this," I said, and started to walk away.

Creole wrapped his hand in mine. "I've already made up my mind, just waiting on you."

I tried to evade his hand but he held on tighter. "I'm supposed to be discouraging fraternization."

"Too damn bad," he growled.

Doc sat at one end of the table with Mother seated next to him, and had his hand over hers. He spied her cigar holder, taking a look inside. "These aren't good for you." He put them out of her reach on the countertop behind her head. Her mouth snapped open and then shut and bit back what had been on the tip of her tongue. Brad watched from behind with a smirk.

Brad took orders and filled everyone's plate with a skewer of fish or shrimp and fresh grilled vegetables, putting the other side dishes in the middle of the large table. Looking back, the large, oblong teakwood patio table had been a good purchase. Bigger is indeed better, since we could all sit together. With a fisherman in the family, fish is about all this family eats. Julie once again made sure everyone had what they wanted. Brad put his arm around her and they kissed.

Doc cleared his throat. "Thank you for inviting me. I find your mother very charming and I hope to spend a lot of time together." He constantly touched her in little ways that had started to make her jumpy.

Brad spoke up, a pleased look on his face. "Mother and Doc make a cute couple, don't they Madison?"

"Mother looks great anytime." I didn't have the nerve to look her way.

Brad, annoyed with me, turned his attention to Creole. "What are your intentions toward my sister?"

"I'd like to know the same thing," Didier spoke up.

I almost choked on my iced tea. "Brad Westin," I hissed. "It's none of your business." I glared across the table at Didier.

"I already told Madeline I'd take her as-is, no returns." Creole stared back at Brad.

"I'm surprised Mother didn't book the wedding the next day," Brad huffed. "Any ex-wives or children you've forgotten to disclose?"

"Three wives and six children."

I squeezed his leg under the table, happy he didn't take anything off Brad.

"How long were you married? Ten minutes?" Liam asked.

Julie shushed him.

"Mom, don't you think he's young for all those wives?" Liam asked.

"I have an ex-husband," I said lamely.

"I'm good with this one, sis. He fits in." Brad

winked at me. "Good luck, dude. She's going to drive you crazy and here's a free tip—Westin women don't listen."

Mother, clearly not happy, snapped, "Brad stop. Madison and I spoke earlier and they're just friends. Nothing else!"

Fab reached her fork across the table and helped herself to a grilled green pepper off my plate.

I smacked her fork away and pointed to the vegetable platter in the middle of the table. "Whatever you want, the answer is yes."

"Oh good, you're still feeling guilty about lying to me." She gave me an evil little smile.

"You lied to your best friend?" Liam said in a stage whisper.

Creole whispered, "I don't tolerate lying. I don't lie and expect the same in return."

"She overworks that angle and so does her boyfriend." I glared at the two of them.

They could've cared less that they annoyed me. Didier chuckled and put his arm around Fab, pulling her close. She made a face.

"What's the case?" I asked.

"Missing cat," Fab managed to say with a straight face.

She clearly wanted to make a scene and I wasn't taking the bait. She'd never take an animal case. I ignored her and turned to Creole.

Liam spoke up. "Career day at school is coming up and I want you and Fab to come talk to my class."

"No, Liam," Julie said a little harshly. "Those two get into too much trouble."

Liam took it in stride, looking upset but never

saying a word, a credit to his mother. Brad and I would've badgered ours until we were sent to our rooms.

"Sometime as hard as we try, the unexpected does happen," I said to Liam. "I wouldn't want to make it sound cool that people sometimes get hurt." I pretty much knew Julie would never allow Liam to accompany me on a job, even a missing cat job. I realized that I might just enjoy being the mother of a teenager and it came as a pleasant surprise.

Fab stood up. "Great food as usual, bro." She leaned down and kissed Brad's cheek. "We're going to sneak off and do naughty things." She linked her arm through Didier's.

"What kind of stuff?" Liam said, clearly excited by the idea.

"Ignore her. She makes stuff up, too." I raised my brows at Julie over his head, she should be happy I put an end to any sex talk.

"Tomorrow, early," Fab said, as she scooted around the table. "We've got stuff to do." She leaned over and whispered, "Don't think I won't send Didier to find you if you get petulant and think you're going to change your mind." Her laugh trailed behind her.

Fab ran around and kissed Mother's cheek, and then she and Didier cut around the pool and down the stairs to the beach.

"What's that French bastard doing in your bedroom?" Creole growled.

I leaned in and almost kissed his lips, catching myself and drawing back. "Calm down, he's never been in my bedroom and is not ever going to be."

"You could've kissed me. You wanted to," he said

gruffly. "Next time, there will be no almost." He pulled me out of my chair. "I've got to go buy some drugs. Set a date for our dinner."

"You need to think about what I said. Don't tell me you weren't listening or don't remember, that would start a fight."

He kissed me hard on the lips and slid his fingers under my bathing suit bottom and pinched me. He hugged Mother and shook Doc's hand. "Welcome to the family," he told Doc.

Doc held out his hand to Mother, she stood and he laid a big kiss on her lips. "Thank you for including me, this has been fun." Mother walked him to the door.

I arched my brows at Brad. "You should have chosen someone far more irritating than kindly Doc Rivers; you know the kind of men she picks for me."

Mother returned and stood at the French doors. "Okay, I get it, no more fix-ups. I liked Doc, although he's bossy. During dinner I confessed that I wasn't available and told him that I was dreadfully sorry that my children used him to punish me for my meddling behavior."

"Couldn't you go out on one date before deciding to be exclusive?" Brad asked, annoyed.

"I told Doc about Spoon and he told me he knew and liked him." Mother frowned at Brad. "Besides, he doesn't tolerate cigars and the loss of them caused momentary panic, but he handed me back my holder at the front door."

Julie put a slice of key lime pie in front of me. She made a raspberry sauce for the plate and added whipped cream. I wanted to lick my lips.

"It's not too late to give Brian a chance, I could

call him," Mother said. "You'd find that the two of you have a lot in common. Can you say that about Creole?"

"Who? NO!" I shook my head. "You got your way Mother; I told him I wouldn't be using him for sex." I tried to sound casual but I'd had enough of the Creole lecture. "If it's the grandchildren issue again, get Brad and Julie to procreate." I winked at Brad.

Julie, blue eyes as big as saucers, made a face at Brad and nodded her head in Liam's direction, who hadn't heard a word, too busy on his phone.

"Are your eggs still good?" I asked Julie.

Liam looked up. "We didn't bring eggs," he said, looking around. "What are you two talking about?"

Julie's cheeks burned and she put a finger to her lips.

I laughed and grabbed my key lime pie and went into the kitchen where I could run my finger around the plate, catching every drop of the yummy sauce.

Chapter 16

Fab screeched into a parking space in front of The Bakery Café. "I've got this crappy job that should have gone to you."

"A freebie?" Fab hated that I regularly took cases from people who couldn't pay, she continually reminded me her half of the partnership wants cash.

"I don't do free. We both get paid."

"Ah, Brick. What does he want?" I wouldn't admit this, but it excited me to think about working for Brick again.

"Brick's niece, Lina Famosa, recently broke up with her boyfriend and since she owned the house, she had him forcibly removed and his belongings followed. Lina believes he came back and stole her cat. Butthole feigned ignorance with one of Brick's men, but prepared himself for a visit armed with a gun."

"I don't think that's his real name." Some days it's just too much fun to annoy Fab. "You owe me." I turned and saw Zach sitting at a table rolling small die cast cars across the table top. Father and son smiled at one another in mutual admiration. Zach looked completely at ease; he'd stepped into fatherhood effortlessly. He looked up and saw me observing them. He nodded but looked uncomfortable to see me.

Fab jerked on my arm. "We're taking our order to go." She placed the order, knowing not to skimp on the whipped cream on my caramel coffee.

I forced myself to turn away. "Why do people think it's okay to dump a pet outside? The cat could have wandered off and gotten lost."

"Lina says Pussy ruled the house and never went outside. She came home and the window was propped open, says she never opens them because she's too lazy to get screens. She's certain the fur ball couldn't open it himself." Fab handed me a picture.

The thought of not having screens made me shudder; it was like a welcome mat to bugs. "Black and white short hair, good-sized cat." I flipped the picture over. "Says here the cat's name is Foster, not Pussy." I tried not to smile. "First stop: the boyfriend's house. I have religious pamphlets in the back. We'll save his soul and snoop around."

"Tolbert told me you fixed him up with some old men friends. Why can't I think of stuff like that?" Fab asked.

"Maybe because you don't know any old men." It would be mean to laugh, her face serious. Fab had forged a tight bond with the preacher.

"They converged on him at the farm, insisted he join them in their weekly lunch and a friendly game of cards afterward. Tolbert said they wouldn't take no for an answer and blackmailed him by saying how upset you would be if he didn't go."

"I don't care how they got him out of the house. He can't sit there by himself all day with no friends. It's not like any of those men are felons."

Fab bumped her way off the highway and across the gravel into the driveway of Lina's ex, Earl Buck. It was a small, weathered white shotgun-style home that termites had treated like a buffet. It suffered from dry rot, and stuck in the middle of an acre or more, it looked lonely without a single tree or plant and no protection from the sweltering heat.

"Hard to tell if anyone's home." I glanced around and spotted a junker car that looked like it hadn't been driven in ages, along with what appeared to be a motorcycle under a tarp and a large pile of bicycles in varied states of disrepair.

The only things on the front porch that looked used were the stairs. A full ashtray sat on the top step; one old, useless beach chair sat alone, the webbing for its seat lying on the ground. I fanned the pamphlets in my hand.

"Get up here," I whispered to Fab. Before I could reach for the bell, the door opened.

"You friends of Earl's?" A girl not far past her teens stared with big brown clouded-over eyes, stringy hair and the scent of weed floating out the door.

I changed my game plan on the spot. "We're looking for Foster. You give us information and you'll get money for junk food."

"Earl would kill me if I told anyone what he did." She clamped her hand over her mouth, her eyes filled with fear.

"I won't be telling Earl anything if you start talking." I channeled my mother's tone of voice that went with the "you're in trouble now" look.

She stepped back. "I didn't have nothing to do with getting rid of Foster," she whined. "I wanted to keep him."

"Is he dead?" Fab demanded.

"He might be by now." Tears leaked from the corners of her eyes. "Earl took Foster to an animal shelter and wanted him put to sleep immediately, but accidently let it slip that it wasn't his cat. Then he made up a story about Foster being a stray. They told him they had a five-day waiting period and he got mad. They kicked him out and demanded he leave or they'd call the sheriff. Earl's scary when he's mad. I usually hide."

"Do you know which shelter?" I asked.

"I didn't go with him. When he got back he screamed over the wait, saying he should've done it himself, put a bullet in Foster's head. How much money do I get?"

I walked back to the SUV, grabbing my purse for cash. I didn't have a good feeling about a happy ending for Foster. I returned and handed the girl the money.

"And you promise not to tell Earl? He can be real mean, although he's always sorry after."

"You'll never see us again." I jumped off the steps and started formulating the next plan of attack.

"That was too easy," Fab said.

"The money I just gave her is an expense, in addition to our fee. Don't forget when you submit your invoice." I reached for my phone to find the closest shelter; nothing within twenty-five miles.

Fab's phone rang and she glanced at the screen. "What's up?"

If that were my call, she'd insist on listening in and had me trained to put it on speakerphone. I snapped my fingers so I could hear, but she ignored me.

"Keep me informed on what she's up to." Fab hung up. "Violet is making inquiries about selling an antique gun collection. Good thing Waynelle and I already talked about these guns of mine."

"You're going to make me ask? Who?"

"Gun dealer friend. I told him about Gus's guns and it just so happens he has intimate knowledge of a couple of them, as he brokered the transaction. I have a little confession: on the way out of Tucker's office, I lifted the envelope Gus left me. Inside I found a key, combo, and the exact location of the safe. I wonder if the reason he didn't leave everything to his daughter was because he knew she's such a devious bitch. Waynelle also told me she wanted a referral to a locksmith; she claimed the guns needed to be inventoried for probate."

"You couldn't steal my envelope, too?" I squinted at her. "How are you going to stop her? I'd bet they'll be moved quickly."

"Gus's house is a couple of exits up. Let's check it out."

"Then after we get the Hummer washed, we can check out the rest of the property mentioned in the will."

"I can't believe you let Apple and Angie touch my SUV." Fab wrinkled her nose.

"If I'm sharing the SUV, I want keys to your Mercedes." I almost laughed at the look on her face; if correctly interpreted, it said, "Hell no."

"I'm tired of your inability to share," I said. "And in the future, if I can't listen in to your phone calls, then mine are off-limits, too."

The traffic light turned yellow; Fab took the time to smirk at me and then gunned it through the intersection. I resisted the urge to scream at her and instead ignored her, knowing full well it bothered her more.

"They do an excellent job because I'm a great tipper and require no sexual servicing."

"Is it too late to wash my ears?" Fab stuck her tongue out.

It surprised us both when we turned off the highway to Pigeon Key and found Gus's driveway roped off with cones and an armed rent-a-guard on duty. Fab slowed to just under the speed limit for once in her driving career and cruised slowly past the property. She made a U-turn, drove back, and pulled up alongside the security car, rolling her window down. "Do you know where the nearest gas station is?"

He swaggered over; Fab had that effect on men. His flirting skills were amateurish, and he gave the slowest and most detailed answer ever. Finally she thanked him and rolled up the window.

"Really, Fabiana? That was excruciating. You couldn't hurry him along, or did you enjoy him looking down your top?"

"While he was preoccupied I scoped out the property. He's the only one on duty."

I rolled down the window, looking out at the ocean that stretched for miles, the breeze rustling through my hair, breathing in the salt air. If only Gus Ivers had a reputable attorney, one who would put a stop to whatever Violet's childlike brain had concocted. Knowing Tucker, it wouldn't surprise me if he had a hand in whatever she had planned to ensure she didn't have to share the estate.

Chapter 17

"You will pull into Clean Bubbles or pull over and I'll drive," I ordered.

Fab glared at me and cut across two lanes into the driveway. Angie hung inside the window of a pick-up truck talking to a guy. She stuck her arm out and waved, her T-shirt soaking wet, and plastered to her ample-sized chest. She wolf whistled and Apple hustled around the side of the building.

I jumped out and Fab reluctantly followed. "You got anything new for me?" I asked Apple.

"You sure know how to pick crap tenants," she said. "Angie," she yelled, "I need help."

Apple smelled like beer and still managed to talk and wash the car in front of her at the same time. "Ron, your new tenant, got arrested at the music festival over the weekend." She pulled her stringy brown hair off her neck into a ponytail.

That even got Fab's interest; she stopped grumbling and stepped forward to hear every word. "For what?" she asked.

"Selling an eight ball at the gate to an undercover cop. Kathy and Ron like their blow. He got cuffed and carted to a booking bus; you have to wait until it gets half full and then they transport to the jail."

Angie stuck her head in the window, still washing the outside. "Did you know Kathy used to be a cop?

That's what she says, anyway. More likely arrested a few times and knows her way around the legal system."

I shook my head. "Ron still in jail?"

"Kathy got his father to bail him out the next day. Only reason he did that is he needs Ron on the job, or he'd have to stop drinking in the middle of the day and maybe put in a full day's work." Apple pulled a cigarette out of her pocket, sticking it in her mouth and puffing.

Should I tell her she forgot to light the thing?

"Anything else?" I didn't want to snap at them, but this whole story made me sick. I knew something was up with that couple and had ignored the warning signs.

Apple shook her head. "I met Joseph's girlfriend. She's pretty. The only thing that bothers me is that she doesn't talk."

Fab hit me on the back; happy I hadn't left my dark black sunglasses in the SUV, they hid my shocked expression. "Can you find out anything and everything on Ron and Kathy and get back to me?"

Angie had climbed inside the car and was polishing the interior. She poked her head out the window and asked, "The more info we get you, the more we get paid?" she asked.

Fab snorted.

"Yes, but it better not be made up." I frowned. "What do you two know about the trailer park?"

"Professor Crum is seriously weird. He runs the place and you better follow his rules. I'd stay away from there; he doesn't allow trespassing," Apple said. "He's a retired college professor from some big deal school in California. Now he's senile and scary."

Just great. "I'm going to go introduce myself. If

105

you hear screams, call the police."

"Can we get paid first?" Angie asked, holding her hand out. Fab growled at Angie and she jerked her hand back inside the car, rolling up the window.

"This might not be a good idea," Fab said as we stared at the trailer park.

"What could go wrong with two girls, two guns, and a senile college professor?"

"Have you noticed every time we say that we get shot at?" Fab grumbled.

The sign over the arbor entrance read, "Tarpon Cove Court. Keep out. Dog gonna eat you," and gun signs littered the rest of the fencing. A beanpole of a man leaned against a tree just inside the court. Towering over six foot, his gray hair stood on end, arms stiff at his side with hands balled into fists; he glared at us. He dressed up for our impromptu visit in his jockey shorts and calf-length rubber boots.

I walked the block. Fab refused to leave the SUV behind in case we needed a quick getaway and parked in front of the fence. "Professor Crum? I'm Madison Westin, I came by to introduce myself. I've inherited the property from Gus Ivers."

"I know who you are. You hired those two trollops over at the car wash that shake their asses all day for money." He looked down his rather aristocratic-shaped nose. "Who's your friend hiding behind your skirt? Nice legs." He ran his eyes over my body. He might be one hundred but he liked to look—and did so leisurely.

Fab stepped beside me, brandishing her Walther, sticking it in the front of her jeans.

"You must be the one Ivers wanted to bang if he

could've gotten the job done," Crum said, raking his eyes over Fab. "I know all about you two. Ivers really wanted the both of you rolling around in his double bed."

After I recovered from my shock, I almost laughed. "How many people live here?" I asked, politely.

"I'm the only occupant, manager, and have a lifetime lease, so good luck getting rid of me." He swept his arm wide, indicating I should go first. "I'll give you a tour. There are twenty five spaces, and five come with broken down trailers."

The only reason I put one foot in front of the other was because I knew Fab, who walked behind the professor, wouldn't hesitate to shoot him; a bullet to the butt would stop him. I hoped he owned more than one pair of underwear.

The outside looked dilapidated and in need of leveling. My heart sunk at the condition of the inside courtyard. I loved a good fixer-upper, but this depressed me. Why own property if you're not going to fix a damn thing? I remembered the sentimental attachment Gus had to Clean Bubbles, maybe it had been the same for the rest of the block.

I waved to a rather large cement hole in the ground and asked, "What was that?"

"Swimming pool. Took years for it to start crumbling and fall apart. Ivers didn't believe in repairing anything. He squeezed hard on to every penny, bent on taking his money to the grave; wonder if he's enjoying it now?"

Crum had a lot of nerve to insinuate that Ivers was cheap; surely, a retired professor didn't have to live like this, except at his own choice. "What's with the two junk cars?" Both Cadillacs were completely stuffed front to back and side to side with an assortment of bottles, cans, and newspapers, and more littered the top. Only the driver's seat of the second car had been spared as a trash receptacle.

"Those are both antique automobiles, my dear, and they belong to me. Do you have no appreciation? I made my home in the one for years and now use it for errands, as I have my trailer for sleeping." He pointed to a rusty pink Air Stream that sat at the back the property, the only one with patio furniture, which consisted of an old glass-top dining table, uncomfortable looking chairs, and a fifty-year-old tabletop barbeque. Not being trailer savvy, I guessed the age to be old, made worse by neglect. I looked around and noticed the sadly neglected plants. The only things that survived were a handful of cactus and some aloe. Although the place looked abandoned, the professor kept it clean of debris.

Fab cleared her throat. "Is it legal for you to strut around in your underwear?"

He swept his hand across the front of his body. "As you can see, I'm clothed in the right place, front and back." He turned to show her.

"Why are the two trollops afraid of you?" I asked.

He grumbled something under his breath. "They tried to squat here one night. Ran their asses off but not before one of them, blurry-eyed drunk, decided to launch herself at me, screaming gutter language."

"Did you hurt her?" I would've loved to have seen that spectacle.

The professor snorted. "I simply moved; she ran into the fence and passed out. Her girlfriend slapped her awake and drug her to the beach for a sand nap."

"This place is disgraceful and I'm not sure what my plans will be, but I'm not going to be a slumlord. Of course, I'd like my lawyer to take a look at your lifetime contract." I gave him a taste of his own behavior and looked down my nose at him. Two can play the snob game.

He looked me straight in the eye. "Slow down, sister. You're not the owner yet, and if Violet Ivers has anything to do with it, you never will be. She has plans for the entire property, including the car wash that she wants back."

"All Violet can do is slow the process and spend a lot of money on attorney fees," I said. Truth: I didn't really know what she could accomplish.

Fab caught the professor's attention by looking him over in the same disrespectful way he did her and she made it clear he didn't meet her standards. "What do you know about Violet Ivers?"

"I know she's a vicious bitch and used to getting everything she wants. Gus spoiled her rotten and then wondered why she turned out to be a snot-ass. She'll steamroll the two of you." He gave a rusty laugh. "She's already got a developer interested in paying big dollars for this property; the two of them have been here several times, heads together, and he's salivating to sign on the dotted line."

I took one last look around and shuddered. The professor walked us around the place, closely watching my response. He had perfect posture and stood ramrod stiff, shoulders back. Fab, who had already deemed him not much of a threat and apparently not worthy of shooting, not on this visit at least, had wandered off a couple of times looking into the windows of vacant trailers and any cranny she felt needed closer inspection. The professor cleared his throat a couple of times, a signal for her to join us, and she ignored him. I kept walking, forcing him to choose between us; he couldn't guard us both.

He walked us back to the gate and flicked his fingers toward the signs. "Since you don't own the place yet, you best heed the very visible warnings."

"When I do take over as owner, you'll need to wear pants, skirt, whatever," I informed him.

"You going to come dress me?" He winked.

I got in the passenger seat and hit the door locks before putting my hands over my face. "Reassure me that place wasn't as bad as it looked."

"Worse."

"Why can't it be like one of the other ones around, shuffleboard court, a pool filled with water, and nice older people playing cards?"

"You forgot to mention clothed. You know he wiggled his ass at me?"

"I want to go home," I whined. "Sit by the pool, have Didier bring us cold water."

"You won't be able to ogle my boyfriend; he's in Miami for all-day meetings. I bet Creole would bring you a bottled water in his teeth." She looked at me. "What's up with you two and why haven't you shared?"

"Mother is dead set against a hook up and has made it clear we are to stay away from one another. She likes the family unit the way it is and doesn't want it all messed up if acrobatic sex turns ugly."

"Toward the end of your relationship with Zach, all you wanted was midnight sex and the occasional date. Is that what you want from Creole?"

I used to love waking up in the middle of the night to find that Zach had slid beneath the sheets, pulling me close. We slept well together, legs hooked over one another. "Creole already told me he's insulted at the sex-only suggestion."

"He's hot, smart, sneaky as hell, and has a good job—you won't have to support him. He's not a criminal, and so what if people think otherwise? He loves your family and tolerates me, your best friend. Did you forget your Aunt Elizabeth gave her blessing for a relationship in the journal she left?"

"I like Creole, he's been a good friend and I appreciate that he has helped us out by supplying information on more than one occasion. I have a terrible track record for relationships. How do I tell Mother I don't care about how she feels? If things blew up and he cut off their relationship she'd never forgive me."

"Shoot me now. It's your fault the ex-husband became a drunk? Besides didn't the two of you part as friends? And keep in touch sporadically? Shame on you for not being obedient to Zach." She shook her head. "Take a page from Madeline's bio and sneak around like she did with Spoon." After a pause, she asked, "Can Creole kiss?"

"He's umm…thorough, and he, uh…takes his sweet time; his hands have a tendency to roam to other restricted places until my toes clench hard. When he stops, it takes me a second or two to catch my breath."

Fab pulled into the driveway and put her hand on

my forehead. "What the hell is the matter with you?"

"I need a swim."

"What is she doing here?" Fab pointed.

We caught Violet Ivers with her hands cupped to the kitchen window, looking in.

"Where does she get her clothes?" Fab asked. "I'm not shopping there, ever."

Violet had somehow found an adult-sized cornflower-blue dress with a white pinafore, white tights, and ugly black flats. Her blonde hair was held back with blue kitty clips.

"No idea. How about if I borrow that get-up from her and you surprise Didier with a little dress up?"

A look of horror crossed her face and then she laughed. "Didier would not be amused," she said, in her best imitation. "Let's back out and pretend we didn't see her."

"I want to know what she wants." I opened the door and hopped out. "What's up, Violet?"

Her eyes snapped with anger. "You really don't have any manners, neither of you."

"If you want something, antagonizing us is not a good start," I said.

"I'm here to speak with her," Violet said, and pointed to Fab. "I'd like to come to an agreement regarding the gun collection."

"What do you really want?" Fab asked. "You and I both know I can't make any promises about something I don't have in my possession."

"Do you know where they are? They need to be inventoried for the estate. I thought the information might be in the letter you stole from Mr. Davis's office."

112

"Tucker probably misplaced the envelope and isn't man enough to own up." Fab looked her in the eye. "The first I heard of the collection was at the reading of the will."

"I'd like to keep them in my family, or donate them to a museum perhaps," Violet said.

Her whiney voice made my ears hurt and gave me a headache. "I can assure you, Fab doesn't have the guns."

"How's the car wash going?" she asked. "I expect my check to be on time at the first of every month. I realize it's a cash operation and there's wiggle room."

"If you have any questions about the check paid by the estate, I suggest you call my CPA. I'm sure he can answer your questions," I said.

"Tucker suggested putting a monitor on the property to make sure all the income is accounted for, but I told him that would be an added expense I didn't think necessary. You look like an honest woman." Hard as she tried, she couldn't erase the insincerity from her voice.

"If you have any more questions, why don't you call first?" I said.

"Let's get together for lunch. Who knows, we could become friends." Violet twisted around, looking over the property.

Fab rolled her eyes. "Thanks, but I already have a friend and she's not going anywhere or I'll shoot her."

"I don't think either of us has offered you our condolences. We met your father through Tolbert and we both liked him a lot," I said.

"Thank you." Violet looked at Fab. "We can talk when the estate is settled." She waved and walked to her car parked at the curb.

"She makes my skin crawl," Fab said.

"I do know from past experience that a death in the family brings out the absolute greed in people."

Chapter 18

Taking a sip of orange water, I eased onto the wooden recliner with its colorful overstuffed pillows, enjoying the hummingbirds as they flittered and fed off the planter at the far side of the pool. Jazz lay stretched out alongside my legs. The bright sky boasted not a single cloud, allowing the sun to warm the tropical flowers encouraging them to open and bloom. I loved my home, and truth be told, I never wanted to move, which was a sticking point in my relationship with Zach. The backyard had become my haven, my favorite place to allow me to think, and a swim always cleared my muddled mind.

Fab had poured herself a glass of wine, throwing her towel onto the twin recliner next to mine. "What are you doing about finding that cat?"

"I could ask you the same question." I looked up from my laptop and she made a grunting noise which I ignored. "I made a list of all the animal shelters in the Keys and have called and scanned a photo to four of them and I'm waiting to hear back from the other two. And you?"

"I'm a delegator. The one with the best cat skills wins, and that would be you."

"You've got one cat vote, Jazz adores you. Let's play some pool basketball?"

"Our game's going to have to wait." She inclined her head to the fence. "Do you have your Glock?" she whispered.

Three dark-suited men walked into the backyard, dark hair, and dark sunglasses. In Florida heat only a real bad-ass shows up in a suit and expensive loafers, with gold watches that screamed "look at how much money I spent," rather than telling the time. The leader would be the one front and center; the other two flanked each side and a respectful step behind.

This had to be a first: neither one of us had a gun. I was happy to be sitting down, since no way this would be good news. Fab and I must be in silent agreement as we didn't say a word, waiting on our guests.

"Miss Westin, I presume," the leader said.

I shook my head in agreement. "And you are?"

Fab sat up and the backup on the left pulled his gun, while the other moved his jacket aside to give an ample view of his shoulder holster and rather large cannon, appearing to me to be a Smith and Wesson magnum of a large caliber.

He ignored my question. "I don't take kindly to you murdering one of my associates, Carlos Osa."

"Madison didn't murder him, and it was self-defense." Fab sneered at him.

I don't think it was her words, but rather the tone of her voice and absolute contempt that drew his anger.

"If one more word comes out of that disrespectful mouth of yours, I'll have my man here tie you up and gag you. Understood?" he seethed in controlled anger. "Answer me."

"Yes, I understand," she answered softly.

"Miss Westin, I will ask the questions, you will answer. I issue the orders and you will follow them to the letter. Anything that you don't understand so far?"

"What do you want?" As an afterthought I added, "No." With each step in my direction, fear raced down my spine.

"Your former associate, Jake Ellis, owes me a lot of money and I want every cent back. Since he's fled town and sold his interest in Jake's to you, it is now your debt to pay." He kicked a chair around and lounged back, controlling his anger for the moment, staring at me almost eye level.

"According to my lawyer, none of his gambling debts were secured by the bar." I held tight to any facial emotion.

"Your lawyer is a jackass. Jake negotiated a deal to discharge all of his debt in exchange for the bar. Now you're going to sign it over to me," he growled, his voice carrying authority.

Of course Jake would screw anyone to save his loathsome neck. "I'll need to see the signed contract."

The leader snapped his fingers. "You didn't listen to my rules."

I hadn't noticed that the second man had a briefcase. He snapped open the locks, pulling out paperwork and handing it to the man in charge.

He reached inside his jacket pocket and produced a shiny silver pen, and, placed it on the top of the contract, handing it to me. "Sign by the Xs. There are three, I believe."

"This isn't Jake's contract," I said, trying to skim; too nauseous to concentrate on the legalese.

"Very astute of you. Now sign," he ordered.

"Why would I do this?" I asked.

"Because I'm asking nicely. You can refuse, but then I'll be forced to apply persuasive and painful means until you agree to sign, saying 'please and thank you.' And after that, you'll require an additional pain-filled lesson for wasting my time." He snapped his fingers and the man reached inside the briefcase, removing a pair of cable cutters.

I had heard a vague story once from Jake about the use of the cutters, and their abilities to snap off one finger at a time.

Fab hissed and I knew his threat would be excruciatingly painful, and was to be avoided at all costs. "What assurances do I have that you'll not kill us?" I surprised myself by not emptying the contents of my stomach onto the flagstone.

"My word." He bared his teeth.

I was out of options and I hated this position. I turned to Fab. "I'm sorry," I whispered. "Love you."

She nodded back and mouthed, "Me too."

"That's fucking sweet, now sign. I'm out of patience and you'll find that I'm extremely disagreeable when that happens." The man behind him flexed the pliers open and closed.

I clicked the pen, scanned the page, and signed at the bottom of the first page. I ran my finger over the next couple of pages, speed reading, slowing for legal terms that jumped off the page. "This contract is for the entire block, which I don't own. Jake never had anything to do with Clean Bubbles."

"You will own the block soon enough, thanks to Ivers, and the contract covers those provisions. Consider it payment for interest and my inconvenience."

I wanted to stall for time but to do what? Jazz looked at me and meowed. I ran my hands along his back and, thankfully, he laid his head down and went back to sleep. I flipped to the last page, for the last two signatures. I hoped he would keep to his word and not kill us, barring that a quick bullet beat torture.

"Hey, over here gentlemen." Creole came through the back the same way as my uninvited guests.

The two bodyguards whirled around, brandishing their weapons, and both were shot from different directions. Fab flew off the lounger and inserted her foot in the leader's chest, kicking him backward off his chair, a resounding crack to the back of his head, spattering blood on the cement in more than one place.

Didier came through the French doors, and sat his smoking gun on the patio table. He swooped Fab off her feet and into his arms and pressed her hard to his chest so that all you could see was her long brown hair.

So this is what Creole looks like undercover; I watched as the scruffy-looking thug handcuffed both men on the ground. They screamed when he jerked their arms back. He wore his baseball cap slung low coupled with dark glasses that concealed the rest of his face. His blue jeans and T-shirt were ripped and torn and he had the dirtiest bare feet I've ever seen.

"You'll pay," one of the guys on the ground said. Creole answered with a hard kick to the ribs.

"Fab, call Harder." When she hesitated, Creole yelled, "Now. And speak only to him." He cleared the space between us and pulled me into his arms. "You so owe me," he whispered.

I clung to him. He was lethal and impressive in

action and I liked it. And disappointed, didn't death survivors get kissed? *One of his kisses would distract my mind from the blood trickling down the face of the man lying on the patio.*

Fab handed Creole her phone and he walked away so that no one could hear the conversation. Fab had other intentions, and when she took a step in his direction, Didier drug her back to his side. His blue eyes bore into her and he said something in French, and from the tone of his voice he wasn't kidding around. She stretched up his torso, locking her arms around his neck, and kissed him.

Fab stage-whispered, "I told the woman who answered, 'This is Madison Westin and I need to speak to Harder personally.'"

"You couldn't say Mr. or Detective?" I asked. "If you're going to impersonate me, at least be polite."

"Like he'd take a call from me," she snickered.

I jumped off the chaise and pointed to the ringleader who up until now lay still, but had started to groan and move. "This one's coming around."

This time Didier let Fab go, and she dashed into the house, returning with a pair of cuffs. Creole intercepted her, turned the man over, cuffed him, and left him face down. "Their ride will be here in a few."

"Thanks, Didier," Creole said, exchanging some kind of secret guy code thing back and forth. "He drove up, saw these three prowling around and called. Since I wasn't far away, I cut my business deal short and instructed him to wait. Nice shot, by the way. Who would've thought that a pretty boy such as yourself could shoot and hit something?"

Fab gave Creole the finger. "How dare you," she

said. If Didier hadn't gripped the back of her shirt she'd have launched herself on Creole.

"Cherie," Didier said quietly.

"He insulted you by insinuating you're a sissy." She turned and yelled at Creole. "I don't think so."

Didier turned her face back to his and gave her the biggest smile I'd ever seen out of him, swooping down on her mouth with a crushing kiss.

Two blue jean-clad cops strolled into the backyard, badges hanging from their waist, 9mm Glocks holstered to their sides. They nodded to Creole. They each jerked a man off of the ground and drug them out the side fence. It didn't take long before they were back for the main guy.

"Do I have to worry they'll be back?" I asked Creole. "Why is there no ambulance and a bunch of sheriff cars?"

"The Frank brothers are getting the VIP treatment. We've wanted them, have them, and we're not sharing with locals. They have a laundry list of charges that will keep them in jail for a long time. They're being hand-delivered to Harder at the jail hospital, who's salivating at their arrival," Creole said. "I have to go back to work. Are you okay?" He looked me over.

"I'm fine." I had a really crappy day, and now that the adrenaline had worn off, I turned away, blinking back tears as I walked into the house. Couldn't he just figure out that I needed another hug on his own and not make me ask for it?

I walked into the house, everything eerily quiet. Fab and Didier were nowhere in sight. I grabbed my phone off the kitchen island. "Would you come spend the night?" I started to cry.

Chapter 19

The bedroom door opened. Mother blew in and flopped down onto the bed, hugging me. "The house has never been this quiet. Fab has that ridiculous ribbon on the door knob."

"This has been an awful day. Another brush with death." I put my head on her chest and gave her the gritty details of the trailer park and Professor Crum; saving the best for last—three suited men holding guns to extort me for Jake's old debts, avoiding any details about Creole except to say that he and Didier were life savers.

Mother rubbed my back as I related the details, a super power she'd used since I was a kid to calm me down; works every time, like a kiss to a skinned knee or a cut finger. "Thanks for coming." I kissed her cheek. "Would you go to The Cottages with me? New tenant, new problem."

"I've got my Beretta," Mother said, and patted her purse. "My friend, Jean, got her concealed license and we both take target practice once a week. You should see the instructor, bulging muscles, dimply smile."

"Spoon know you have a wandering eye?"

"You better not tell him," she laughed.

* * *

I cruised into the driveway of The Cottages and drawn

123

into the middle of the asphalt with chalk was a hopscotch diagram; Mac was jumping the squares, Shirl cheering her on, holding a beer.

"Aren't they a little old for that game?" Mother said, watching in fascination. "Their boobs are taking a beating, both of them are under-supported."

A cool breeze blew in off the Gulf as we got out of the SUV, and I surveyed the property. Joseph waved from his chair in front of his door, Svetlana straddling his body. Mother didn't know about the new girlfriend, so I'd have to introduce them and watch her reaction.

Shirl put her arm around Mac. "We're working off nervous energy. Mac thinks you're going to fire her."

"Don't be ridiculous. I'm considering tying Mac to a chair and making her stay here 24/7."

Both of them made faces.

Kathy's red pick-up truck blew into the driveway with her behind the wheel. Two men were crammed alongside her, one being her elusive husband. I waved and walked in their direction. Ron grabbed Kathy's hand and met me halfway.

"This is my husband, Ron," she introduced. To look at them together you'd never guess the twenty-year age difference; drugs had taken their toll on him, and he looked older and haggard.

Ron looked like he'd slept on the beach and was in desperate need of a shower. He mumbled something unintelligible and looked bored. "Nice to meet you," he finally said, like a recalcitrant child. Kathy looked in better shape with a knee-length, form-fitting cotton dress, no underwear, the back tucked between her butt cheeks.

"I just received a phone call from my bank that

your cashier's check is fraudulent," I told her, waiting for a reaction.

Kathy never flinched, showing no emotion, she smiled. "I found out about that myself and I'm on way to the bank." She patted Ron on the shoulder. "I didn't get a chance to tell you, don't worry I'll take care of it."

I found it surprising that Ron, for the first time hearing about a bogus bank check, had no reaction. Kathy had honed her acting skills.

"How did this happen?" I asked. "My bank would like to know the same thing and is investigating."

Ron's phone rang; he looked relieved. Nodding at Kathy, he ran to their cottage and slammed the door.

"He's expecting an important call," Kathy said. "I'll take care of the check today."

"You'll have to pay in cash. And another thing I may have failed to mention, The Cottages has a no drugs policy, unless its prescription, and I don't know of a doctor along the beach that prescribes cocaine."

Her eyes flinched. "Those charges will be dropped before the preliminary hearing; it's a case of mistaken identity. I can assure you that neither of us do drugs."

This woman lied like a second language, very skillfully. I'd bet her hair extensions we didn't know the half of this devious couple.

"If there's going to be a problem with paying your rent I'd appreciate you moving out without any drama. I do have an effective eviction service that bypasses all that pesky legal paperwork."

Her brown eyes hardened. "I'm sure we can work everything out without threats."

Kathy flounced back to her cottage, and once

again, I noticed the price tag hanging from the back of her dress. She must be one of those annoying people who purchased clothing, wore it, and then returned it.

I waved my arms at Mother to join me, and crossed the driveway to where Joseph sat hanging on to every word. "You know, Joseph, I've been amazingly tolerant with all your bullshit since you've lived here, legal and otherwise, and never said no to picking you up at the jail, even in the middle of the night."

"You make my head hurt. What do you want?" he whined, sucking down the last of his beer and crushing the can with his foot.

Mother placed her hand on the small of my back and stroked soothing circles.

I narrowed my eyes. "How about a better attitude and some appreciation? Explain to me how you know nothing about your new neighbors while living directly across the driveway from them. I want to know everything about those two and you're the perfect person to dig up every piece of lint."

Joseph jerked up in his chair and started coughing, running his hand through his dirty, thinning brown hair.

"Mother, I'd like you to meet Joseph's girlfriend, Svetlana." I stepped back, so that she could see the overly endowed, skimpily attired attractive brunette sitting next to Joseph. The last time I'd seen her she'd been a blonde.

Mother stuck her hand out and jerked it back. "This looks like a hum...a...I like her manicure."

"Yes, Mother, Svetlana is an anatomically correct rubber doll."

Mother stared at her another second and then burst out laughing. She turned and continued to laugh, walking back to Mac and Shirl who looked annoyed they hadn't been invited to listen.

I should be nicer to Joseph since the doctors insisted he's half dead, and even as infuriating as he could be, he'd better not die without notice. I'd miss him. "I'll be hearing from you soon?"

"Svetlana and I need a nap." He jerked her up by her arm and disappeared inside his cottage and kicked the door shut.

Mother stuck her fingers in her ears. She didn't appreciate that Miss January sat rocking on her porch belting out an old show tune, Kitty on her lap. I sort of recognized the melody but she couldn't remember all of the words. It didn't help that her electric cigarette wiggled between her lips. Her true desire was to chain smoke, but she managed to stick to a pack a day and sucked on the electric one in between cigarettes.

"We need to have a meeting in the office so no one can hear. You might as well come along," I said to Shirl, "save Mac from repeating everything."

"Shirl's my best friend," Mac said, and pouted.

She unlocked the door and sat at her desk, passing around her stash of bubble gum. It shocked me that Mother took a piece and then dropped it in her pocket.

"Have you seen Svetlana naked?" Mother asked.

"I tried to flip her skirt one day but Joseph started yelling. I looked at the rubber girls online and you can get pretty much anything you can afford to pay for and the body parts aren't cheap," Mac said.

"Meeting comes to order," I said, leaning against the corner of the desk, thinking I needed a gavel or a princess wand. "Kathy will be bringing you cash today for the fraudulent cashier's check and I want a call when it happens."

Mac sat straight up in her chair. "Why didn't I know anything about this?"

"If you didn't know about the check then why am I going to be firing you?" I asked.

Shirl cleared her throat and spoke up. "I just updated her about the late night activity with the new tenants."

I covered my eyes with my hands and shook my head. "Tell me the sheriff hasn't been here?"

"No and not a word of complaint out of the neighbors," Shirl said. "I peek out the blinds and watch the cars come and go, starting about ten and all through the night. Kathy bounced over one night and invited me to dinner, but I turned her down and now she's not all that friendly. No loud music or fights, only the constant traffic in and out."

"Liam told me Kathy and her friends always bring the party to the pool, she gets up early every morning and cleans the area. Bags the beer cans and cigarettes and walks them down the street to someone else's trashcan," Mac said. "I tried to talk to Joseph, since his unit backs up to the pool. He told me to mind my own business, that Kathy and Ron were 'good people.'"

"Kathy walks dinner over to him every night," Shirl said. "I check on him every day to make sure he's still breathing so all I hear is Kathy this and that, and it's annoying."

"Make me a copy of their application, I'll check them out myself," I said to Mac. "Let's hope we can get them out of here before they kill someone." The Cottages had a poor track record in renting to locals, choosing only the ones who turned out to be big bags of trouble.

"Good news is that the other guests like her, she's friendly, flirts with the men when their wives aren't looking, so no complaints." Mac handed me the Stones' file.

"Meeting adjourned." I slipped off the desk top. "Come on," I said to Mother, "let's go get lunch." I decided on a princess wand for the next meeting, now to find one.

Mother looked over to Miss January's cottage. "I think she's probably passed out. At least she's stopped singing."

I looked at my watch. "No worries, she naps every day at this time." I handed my phone to Mother. "Let's call in a take-out order."

* * *

Fab—in a silk deep-purple teddy, trimmed in wide black lace—came rushing into the kitchen where Mother and I sat finishing our pizza and salad. Didier was right behind her. He had on black silk pants and a short-sleeve silk shirt, must be date night. She hugged Mother and asked me, "Why aren't you getting dressed?"

"I'm not the one in my underwear," I said.

"Hurry up. Didier hates to be late," Fab said. "Did you forget the opening of Rockstar in South Beach?" It was the newest happening in-spot to be seen and charged obscenely high prices for drinks.

"No, I didn't forget because you didn't invite me." I held up my hand. "Stop. I won't bore you with an elaborate excuse. Not going."

Mother patted my arm. "Sounds like fun, you might meet someone. I'll go home and you can call me in the morning, tell me all about it."

Didier arched his brow at Fab. "Well I thought I told her," she mumbled.

"I'd rather spend the evening with Mother. I'm in need of spending money, so I'll be cleaning her out after a few friendly games of poker."

Mother winked. "I may let you win a hand."

"Bring me back a pair of blinking flip-flops," I said.

The South Beach sidewalks were crammed with entrepreneurs selling anything they could find that lit up along with all the usual tourist stuff.

"Don't forget your appointment in Brick's office tomorrow," Fab said, and shook her finger at me. "Fresh start. You don't bring up old news and he won't either. You two are to kiss and make up because I don't want another cat case."

"That's another thing you failed to mention." I frowned at her.

"This I thought was better to spring on you last minute. You're not telling your very best friend no, are you?" She stared at me.

Didier tapped his watch. "Get dressed, Cherie." He kissed Fab and she ran upstairs.

"Thank you for being more gracious than the last time," I said to Didier.

He put his arm around Mother, drawing her into a hug and kissing her cheek. He said to me, "You seem to have overcome most of your whininess." His mouth curved up. "But don't think I won't hesitate to use my high-handed techniques again."

Fab glided back into the kitchen in a very short deep-purple V-neck dress the same shade as her teddy. Fab and Didier were a show stopping couple, both with their dark good looks and that mysterious air about them.

We watched them leave. "Why didn't you go?" Mother lightly pinched my arm.

"I like dive bars, hamburger stands, and flip-flops. Fab does the dress up and stiletto heels, she speaks French, and professes to love caviar. The look of it makes me keep my lips tightly closed."

Mother clasped my face in her hands. "I've seen you do dressed up and with your amazing red hair, you are every bit as sexy. You remind me every day of my mother."

I blew her a kiss. "I wish I'd known her." I smiled. "So how much cash do you got on you?"

Mother filled a glass with her favorite, Jack, and added a couple of ice cubes. "Let's go out on the patio, so I can savor a cigar while the queen shows you how the game is played."

Chapter 20

Mother and I went downstairs early in the morning, passing by Fab's door; the ribbon firmly in place, we giggled like schoolgirls. One of my black dresses hung on a cabinet knob, low-heeled slides on the countertop, along with a note in Fab's handwriting. I read it aloud to Mother.

Brick has a delivery job for a special client and he wants you dressed up for the job. Wear what Didier picked out. He said to put your hair up, too. You'll be leaving immediately from Brick's office.

"Do you suppose he picked this out?" Mother held in her hand my black lacey strapless bra that I'd only worn once.

"Oh, I hope that was Fab's contribution." I blushed.

"When is he going to come dress me?" Mother asked.

* * *

Since Brick and I had a disagreement about my unwillingness to help evict senior citizens, it had been a long time since I darkened the doors of Famosa Motors. He thought he could trick me, and when that didn't work, he ordered me; he turned out to be wrong on both of those ideas.

Brick had his checkbook in a lot of what most people would call "interesting" businesses. He owned multiple pawnshops, a bail bonds business, a private investigation firm, and The Gentlemen's Club—also known as a strip club—out in Alligator Alley.

Bitsy, his receptionist, sat at her desk in front of the roll-up doors. Brick had transferred her from his Gentlemen's Club to Famosa's saying she'd be good for business with her bubbly personality and voluptuous curves always on display. She had a side business selling information, but the problem was that if a higher bidder came along, she'd screw the first customer. She labored under the misconception that because she worked for Brick, she had carte blanche, but one of these days she'd cheat the wrong person and receive a painful lesson or worse.

"Mr. Famosa is expecting you," Bitsy said as soon as she saw me.

"Nice hair." I wanted to laugh at the look of outrage on her face. She knew that I knew her mane of long blonde hair was a wig because I'd had an occasion to rip it off her head, having been one of her disgruntled customers.

"I can do this," I whispered when I got to the top of the stairs. Didier made a good choice, I thought, looking down at my black scoop-neck dress, which hit me mid-thigh, and my bare tan legs in red slip-on heels. I stood at the door of his office and waited until he got off the phone, enjoying the view from his second-floor window.

Brick hung up and motioned me in. "Very nice." His dark eyes did a slow sweep of my body. "I'm happy you came." He gestured to a chair in front of his desk.

"Why me for the job? Fab's skills far exceed mine." I looked him in the eye to detect any hint that I should run.

"Fab's easily excited; the next thing you know guns come out and someone is dead." He finished off his bottled water, indicating his well-stocked refrigerator and that I could help myself.

He continued. "You have people skills and that's what this job requires. Your job is to escort a flatbed with a Rolls Royce Phantom sedan to my client's door on Hibiscus Island. You will see that it is unloaded where directed, and then be escorted by a bodyguard into the house of my client, Carmine Ricci. Leave your gun in the glove compartment. Although Carmine will admire your obvious charms, there will be no problems. You will present the paperwork to him, and have him sign in the places indicated. Present this silver Mont Blanc pen for him to use and he is to keep it when finished. He will also be giving you a check."

"Can you promise me nothing will happen, such as getting shot or going to jail?"

"This is a straight up business deal and if it goes well, I will use you for other high-end deals. Carmine is rich, he's not coming here to sign paperwork. He'd much rather have a pretty, sexy woman come to him. He won't touch you because he knows I'll cut his arms off."

"You're assuring me the job is as described and there are no unpleasant things you failed to mention."

"I swear." He held up his hand. "You know I'm a man of my word. When finished, bring the paperwork to the W Hotel in South Beach where I'll be having lunch."

He handed me a black leather portfolio.

I opened my purse, took out a piece of paper, and pushed it across the desk. "I found Foster. He'd been rescued from the animal shelter where the dirtball boyfriend took it to be put to sleep. Clever bastard dropped it off in Homestead thinking it would never be found. Thank goodness they had a waiting period. I faxed the photo to the animal shelter, and they knew the woman who rescued him and referred me on. Your niece should be having a happy reunion soon. Animal Rescue would like a donation and I told her a check would in the mail by tomorrow and, if not, to call me back."

He opened his side drawer and withdrew an envelope, handing it to me.

"Does that include the bribe money to get info out of the new girlfriend? We no longer incur bribery expense; it's billed back to the client."

"You're ballsy, Red."

Brick only called me by the nickname he gave me when he wasn't mad.

"By the way, in the future, I'm your girl for all animal cases."

He laughed. "Here's an update for you that you're bleeding heart will probably like, none of the seniors were forced to move out. I hired a company to relocate them to a place they can afford." He handed me a set of keys. "The flatbed is loaded, Henry's driving. The guard at the island gate is expecting you. If you have a single hiccup, you call me."

* * *

135

I agreed to follow Henry out to Hibiscus Island, located in the Biscayne Bay. The drive over the causeway was breathtakingly beautiful; the highway ran over the turquoise water below, passing by other small islands.

I arrived at the man-made oval-shaped island which had amazing water views and very visible security. I rolled down my window at the guard station and he politely informed me that Mr. Ricci was expecting me. He directed me straight ahead, and before driving away, I withdrew a photo of the house from the portfolio. Brick thought of everything. The gates at the end of the driveway stood open, so I pulled in. Another guard stood just inside the gates of the two-story estate. He walked up to the window, checked me over, and waved me through, directing me to park at the front door where a well-dressed gentleman waited. I walked over to him and asked where he'd like the Rolls parked. He indicated they'd take possession once it rolled off the truck. I waited patiently while the Phantom was unloaded, afraid to walk away but unsure what I would do if it fell off the back end. I laughed to myself.

The second guard stood next to me, never saying a word. I breathed a sigh when the Phantom offloaded without a hitch.

"Mr. Ricci is waiting," the man said, motioning me forward.

He led me from the entry way. Looking around, I guessed the house to be about ten-thousand square feet, and was happy that cleaning it wasn't my responsibility. Mr. Ricci's mansion held an impressive collection of antiques, mixed in with modern and avant-garde artwork. Nothing about the house said "comfortable and homey."

He stepped aside, motioning me into the formal living room that boasted an expansive water view of downtown Miami. The guard stationed himself at the double doors.

Mr. Ricci looked comfortable staring out at the water in his over-sized leather chair; looking like a character out of an old gangster movie.

He stood. "Miss Westin, I presume. Lift your dress to the tops of your thighs." He looped his finger, indicating he wanted me to do a full turn.

I hesitated—*damn Brick*—and did as he asked, shoving my skirt back down quickly. Mr. Ricci waved off the guard and he left, closing the door.

"You know, I love redheads," he said.

I blushed and ignored his comment. "You have a beautiful house. I have the paperwork for the Phantom," I said, holding out the portfolio.

He put his hand under my elbow and guided me to the dining table, pulling out a chair. I presented him the Mont Blanc pen. I had already taken a quick peek and wished I could keep it but would be afraid to let it out of my sight.

Mr. Ricci barely looked at the contract. Scanning each page quickly, he signed in the indicated places. Once done, his bodyguard reappeared, setting a briefcase in front of me. Snapping open the locks, he lifted the lid, revealing perfectly organized bundles of one hundred dollar bills.

Is this even legal? What the hell's wrong with a check? I nodded my head, as though I knew what I was doing.

"Would you like to count it?" Mr. Ricci laughed, enjoying his own private joke.

137

"That won't be necessary." I forced myself not to fidget in my seat, laying the contract on top.

The guard snapped the case shut and set the lock.

Mr. Ricci handed me back the Mont Blanc pen. "A gift from Mr. Famosa," I said.

"Brick certainly has good taste." He stripped me naked with his eyes. "I'd like you to stay for lunch."

My cheeks burned. No way, not even if I had to make a run for it; although, I suspected there would be no escape that Mr. Ricci didn't allow. "Mr. Famosa is expecting me and you know how ill-tempered he can become when his orders are not followed."

"We're a lot alike in that way." He extended his hand.

I stared at it. *No*, my brain screamed. I hated shaking hands. Hopefully, my hesitation went unnoticed. He took my hand in his and turned it over, kissing my palm.

"It was very nice meeting you, Miss Westin."

The guard pulled back my chair. "Enjoy your Phantom." I smiled with relief, the front door in sight. He escorted me through the house, opened the door to the Hummer, and stood watching me drive through the gates until they closed behind me. The man never said one word.

Chapter 21

The cutting-edge W Hotel had a five-star rating for a reason. Sitting on the shores of one of the most glamorous beaches, it embraced the lively spirit of the area; international trendsetters set the decadent pace for the rich and famous in South Beach.

The hostess escorted me to Brick's table, which was tucked in an alcove that overlooked the pool. The view of half-naked women swimming under the waterfall below had captured the attention of the four men at the table and they were clearly entertained. I spotted Brick's brother Casio's bald head first, and to hear Casio tell it he's a big deal within the Miami police department. The Famosa brothers were not men to screw with; I'd heard whispers about how bad things can happen but I knew nothing first hand, thank you.

I leaned down and whispered in Brick's ear, "This better be legal." I handed him the briefcase.

Brick unlocked the case and pulled out the paperwork. "You know my brother. The other two are friends." He flipped through the pages. "Everything go okay?"

That was an odd introduction. Both men, dark haired and casually attired all in black, looked like criminals with high priced accessories. They looked me over as though they were purchasing something expensive and didn't want any flaws. "You left out a couple of details, but then don't you always..."

The men at the table laughed.

"Check's in the mail." Brick's eyes twinkled with amusement.

"Nice to meet you, gentlemen." I turned to leave and bumped into Stanhope III.

Walden Stanhope, or The Third, as my brother called him. They'd become best friends in high school and still kept in touch. I had a huge crush on him when he was a senior and fantasized that he'd be the one to take my virginity with all the romance a teenage girl can dream up. But Brad would have none of his best friend "banging" his sister, so I had to wait. In reality, my first time turned out to be awkward and clumsy, better perhaps if I'd done "it" with someone with experience.

"Madison!" Stanhope wrapped me in a bear hug. He stepped back, not letting go of my hand, and spun me around. "You're delicious."

"You're not bad yourself." His black, faintly pinstriped suit fit him well, and being a shoe aficionado, the black leather loafers were a good choice.

"I just picked your brother's pockets clean over a few games of pool before he left on a fishing trip," he said as he steered me over to the bar. "Your name is still off limits. When I ask I get a terse 'fine.' He's still looking out for you. Brad's a good guy."

Stanhope played with the ends of my hair. "I got married, divorced, twin boys, I hope they turn out nothing like me, I'm admittedly an asshole." He looked behind me and smirked. "Let me introduce my associate, Mr. Creole."

Creole also wore a black suit, his hair pulled back

in a short ponytail tied with a leather strip. They both looked like well-dressed criminals. The hotel appeared full of them today, in every corner table conducting business. I ran a leisurely eye up and down and winked. His eyes held a warning. He didn't like that Stanhope had put his arm around me, or that he continued to hold me tightly to his side.

Stanhope said, "This is sweet Madison."

"Keep your hands off, Stanhope," Creole growled and tried to jerk me from his grasp.

Stanhope ignored him, maneuvering me out of his reach. I hoped Creole wouldn't hit him. I told Stanhope, "Mother will be sorry she wasn't here, you should stop by and see her sometime. Take her some of Cuba's finest and she'll never stop talking about you."

He had a deep baritone laugh. "Your mother scares me. Even as a teenager, when Brad and I would get caught doing what we were told not to, she'd call me and tell me to get my ass over to the house and take my punishment, which meant hard labor. The cool thing was that she never once ratted me out to my parents. Then she'd make us clean the garage or something. She'd check on us periodically, bringing cold drinks, and we'd put on our angry, unhappy faces. We were never entirely sure if we had her fooled into thinking that we were doing more horsing around than work."

"Remember when she took a broom and swept you off the front porch, in one sweep? That's what you got for teasing me."

"She started screaming at me, 'You made my daughter cry.' After a couple of smacks to my backside with the bristles of the broom, I ran and didn't come back

141

for a couple of days."

"Nice apology, though, when you did come back; although, I longed for a kiss. I had the biggest crush and there you were, saying the sweetest words."

"You're all grown up now, we should get together some time." Stanhope pulled on a strand of my hair.

Creole pushed him away. "I don't think so. She's got a boyfriend."

Stanhope laughed at him and checked his watch. "We've got another meeting." He hugged me again and kissed my cheek.

"Be careful," I whispered to the two of them.

"Where's my kiss?" Creole asked.

"Last time I saw you, you left me in a weakened state to cry my eyes out." I turned and walked out.

* * *

I slammed the front door, giving Fab and Didier notice that they were about to be interrupted.

"How did it go?" Fab yelled from the living room.

"Except the part where he asked me to lift my dress, looking for a gun I presume, everything went fine. Did you know that would be a request?" I asked her. I could tell by her shocked expression she hadn't had that request yet. I stepped back and lifted my dress in demonstration.

Didier laughed. "I'll bet you charmed him." He handed me a box. "This came for you."

I took the scissors he offered. "Merci for picking out my dress. I've never had so many appreciative stares."

"Do me a favor and clean out your closet, it

borders on a disgraceful mess." He shook his finger. "It won't be so hard to find something next time."

"I know Fab very well and did she clean her closet when you asked so nicely?"

Didier sighed. "No, she didn't. I did it myself."

Fab jerked the scissors away and ripped the box open. She pulled out a black velvet drawstring bag and handed it to me.

I read the note aloud. "Job well done." Untying the bag, I pulled out a sea-green leather clutch and lifted the golden-snap monogrammed closure; inside was Brick's check. "I wouldn't mind more of these jobs. The whole time I was in the presence of Mr. Ricci I felt the protection of Brick."

"This means you two have kissed and made up and we can do jobs together again," Fab said.

"Which one of you picked out the bra?" I asked.

They looked at one another and back at me. Fab said, "You'll just have to wonder, won't you?"

Chapter 22

I snuggled into the warm body next to mine, stretching like a cat. I moaned, opening my eyes, feeling teeth running along my neck. I stiffened and opened my mouth to scream when a hand clamped down. "Don't scream or I'll have to shoot Fab."

"What the hell are you doing?" I hissed, the second he took his hand away. "You cannot come into my bedroom uninvited, in case I wasn't clear the last time." I jerked the sheet up under my neck.

"I came by to tell you how damn sexy you looked yesterday," Creole growled. "One kiss and I'll leave."

I laughed softly. "You abuse the phrase, 'one kiss.' You forget, I agreed to that once already."

"Did you not enjoy it?" He pulled me roughly to him, nibbling my lower lip.

"I don't remember," I lied. "Now leave."

"I didn't like Stanhope's hands all over you." He twisted his fingers in my hair, pulling, making me wince.

"That's a total exaggeration. Were you jealous?" I'd never admit it to him but I liked the idea, even though I shouldn't have.

"You're playing with fire." He bit my neck hard enough to leave a mark.

"I'm not the one sneaking into your bed. You know Mother doesn't approve?"

"We're adults and can decide for ourselves, and I

vote yes. Since when do you do what you're told?" He bit down hard again, eliciting another moan that escaped despite my best effort.

"I can behave, although I don't enjoy it very much."

"Let's put that to a test, shall we?" He rolled over, straddling my body. "I'm tired of waiting, so tell me yes or I will use every unfair advantage to coerce you into saying, moaning, or screaming yes." He pulled the sheet away. "You're wearing my shirt. It looks better on you than me. You know it's my favorite shirt now."

After the barbeque, I came up to my bedroom to find a dress-shirt and T-shirt neatly folded on my bed with a sticky bow. I knew without a note they belonged to Creole; his scent still lingered on the fabric. He didn't like the idea that the shirt I wore the last time he sneaked in might have belonged to another man. I had no intention of telling him that I had worn his shirts every night since then.

"Don't you have to go to work?"

He looked at my bedside clock. "I've got a couple of hours."

I groaned inside. I'd never be able to hold out for hours. "Get off me. If you can behave yourself, you can catch a quick nap."

"And then I get my one kiss!" He rolled off, pulling me into the spoon position, throwing a thigh over my legs.

Why can't I just whisper yes? You know you want to.

* * *

145

Fab squinted at Creole. "How long have you been here? And how did you get in?" she demanded when we walked into the kitchen in search of coffee.

"How did you get past the guard dog?" I asked.

"Yeah," Fab said, not happy. "Now that you two are sleeping together, when are you going to start telling everyone you're a couple?"

I glared at her. "We are not doing anything and don't you tell anyone anything to the contrary."

Fab rolled her eyes. "Your hair is a mess, your lips look swollen, and you're wearing a shirt with his name on the back. And I bet you're naked under it. And nothing happened. Oh, okay."

Didier laughed, he clearly didn't believe my explanation either.

Creole had given me his quarterback jersey from when he played football at the University of Miami. He stroked my hair, working on a knot.

"Stop it." I jerked away. Little good that did me, he jerked me back and continued to untangle the knot using his finger.

"Does Creole remind you of anyone you know?" I looked at Didier.

"You and I will have a talk later," he informed me and smiled.

Oh, great. That didn't sound fun. I'd be avoiding Didier like he had crabs.

"I need your help today," Fab said.

"I've got a busy schedule." I looked her in the eye which sold a lie faster than fidgeting around.

She narrowed her eyes. "What?" she demanded.

"Ask me again later and by then I will have thought of something."

Creole laughed. "Good one."

"You're not the least bit funny. We'll leave after you get rid of lover boy," Fab said, glaring at Creole.

"Ignore her, she's irritable because this is the second time you've snuck into the house right under her nose." I grinned at her.

Fab prided herself on her security guard skills where the house was concerned; no one had ever been able to sneak past her before. Creole now put two blemishes on her perfect record.

He leaned across the counter, getting into her face. "Do not upset Madison."

I smirked at Fab, knowing she and Didier liked Creole and wanted me to stop being so indecisive when they were both certain I liked him back.

Creole put his coffee mug in the dishwasher. He advanced on me, a fierce look on his face. I thought briefly about running, but I knew how that would turn out—he'd catch me and I'd be lying under his body.

He grabbed my arm. "As of right now, I'm out of patience," he said, and jerked me toward the front door. "She'll be back."

"Where are you taking me, I don't have shoes on." I tried to pull back but he held fast, slammed the door, and pushed me up against it, kissing me.

"Have a good day, honey." He smacked my butt and left.

Chapter 23

"Do you have to have to go to the bathroom?" I asked Fab as she slid behind the wheel.

"Nooo," she said, and glared.

"Just checkin'. Mother never allowed us to get in the car without peeing first."

"My mother never mentioned bathroom habits in her life." Fab rocketed out of the driveway. "I need a triple espresso."

"Is today's job for one of your smarmier clients?"

"No, this is a personal favor. You didn't leave your gun in your underwear drawer, did you?"

I made a face at her and lifted my skirt, my Glock holstered to my thigh. "Hmm…'Personal favor' translates to 'you owe me.'"

"When have I ever said no, unlike you?" Fab asked. "Lately, your stories are not up to your usual high standard."

"My memory is better than yours. In the past I remember having to trick and lie to get you to help me. I'm still the Queen of the Stories."

Fab slid into an available space at The Bakery Café, right in front of Zach and Slice, who were sitting at an outdoor table. "It's not too late to back out and we'll get coffee somewhere else."

"I'm not happy we broke up but I'm very happy Zach Jr. has a hands-on dad. Besides, Slice just waved." I crossed the sidewalk to their table. "Hi, guys."

"I'll be back with your usual, to go," Fab said from behind my back.

"Heard you had a little trouble at your house," Slice said. Zach's partner scared most people by his sheer size, as well as the fierce look on his face. He didn't scare me, but I'd never been on his bad side and he helped me out when I needed muscle.

Zach looked surprised.

"Good news travels through interesting circles; didn't know it was common knowledge."

"It's not, but my connections are impeccable." He bared his teeth, in a Slice smile.

That meant he and the District Attorney were still an item. "The last of Jake's disgruntled business associates, I hope. I'm thinking about a name change."

"That's a great idea." Zach ran his fingers along my arm. "You doing okay?"

"How's fatherhood?" I asked, ignoring his question.

"The three generations of Anthonys got together last weekend for an all-male outing to the Alligator Farm and had a great time. I'm learning more from my son than the other way around." Zach smiled the whole time he spoke, and the hard lines in his face softened.

"I think you'll be an amazing dad," I said, and I meant every word.

"I'm at your service, anytime." Slice hit my arm.

Fab appeared with our coffees and a bag of treats. It was damn near impossible to walk by the bakery case and not want something; they made the most mouth-watering sweet rolls. Mother always bought an assortment.

"Are there two in there?" I pointed to the bag. Fab had the annoying habit of wanting to share.

She rolled her eyes. "We're late. Bye guys."

Zach stood and caught my hand. "I hope we're still friends." He hugged me.

I nodded, unsure of what to say. "Stay safe, both of you."

Fab grabbed the back of my top, jerking me away. "Why do you always have to be so nice? Creole won't like Slice riding to the rescue, think about that before you make the call."

"He won't mind Slice as much as Zach. Tell me about the job."

"You'll see."

I hated those words and gave my Glock a reassuring pat.

* * *

We rode in silence down the Overseas. I stared out the window at the Gulf of Mexico. I realized Creole had been consuming more of my thoughts lately and I smiled at the thought of saying "yes" to him, and then Mother's wagging finger flashed before me.

Fab interrupted my thoughts. "What are you going to do if you drag your feet with Creole until he feels jerked around and is done with you?"

"I'm just scared. All the what-ifs and then there's Mother, who seems so sure we're not a match. I want everyone to be happy."

"Ponder this: if your mother slapped around in

your flops, would she not date someone just because you asked? Brad is proof that the answer is no. He practically begged her to stop seeing Spoon." She held up her hand.

"I'm not finished," she said. "I've seen the way you look at him all breathless and wistful. I know your thoughts are naughty, because your cheeks get flushed when you're lost in thought and you think no one's paying attention, like now."

"I'm happy I didn't give up on you and your negative attitude about being friends."

"Another thing," she said, and shook her finger. "Creole and I get along; he gets me. When I offer up a load of sarcasm he doesn't get all mad and stomp out the door, he serves it back. Did you know that Didier and Creole went for a twenty-mile bike ride? We have the potential for doing something a lot less strenuous as couples."

Fab jerked the wheel and took the exit to Pigeon Key. We bumped over the gravel, and leaving a dust bowl in our wake, we pulled into The Wild Bird Farm, but Tolbert's car was nowhere in sight. Grover must have gone for a ride because he wasn't standing guard on the porch. She drove to the far side of the property and veered off on a dirt side road.

"You're going to get the Hummer dirty," I whined.

"You keep lookout and make sure we don't attract the attention of the guard at the end of the driveway."

I had forgotten that Tolbert's property and Gus Ivers' property shared an access road that ran along the back. We parked on the far side of the two-story Victorian-style house, completely hidden from the road.

151

"This is illegal, Fabiana Merceau."

"We saw a pickup blow out of the back of the property and didn't recognize the driver, came over to investigate, and found the back door open. We're in the process of securing the place."

I wanted to stay put in the SUV with the door locked but got out anyway, despite my better judgment.

"Just checking to see what Violet is up to." Fab slipped her lock pick out of her pocket and tossed me a pair of rubber gloves.

The lock popped in a second and we entered the kitchen. "All's quiet; that's a good sign." Fab looked around. "What do we have here?" She pointed to a stack of boxes lining the wall in the dining room.

To me, the house was dark and dreary and more than a little creepy. I lifted the lid on the nearest box. "Looks like Violet's packing personal mementos."

In the corner sat a large roll-top desk. Someone sitting there could see the comings and goings along the main highway. "She's looking for something," Fab said. "The desk is mostly empty; she upended the contents onto the floor and what she didn't want went into these plastic bags to be dumped."

"Judging by the number of boxes, I'd say she's been busy since his death. Can we leave now?"

"I want to check upstairs and then we're out of here."

I followed her, since there was no way I'd stay behind by myself.

Fab peeked in each bedroom and opened the last door at the end of the hall. An unidentified bald man with a three-strand comb-over pointed a gun in her face.

"You're trespassing," he said as he cocked his gun. "I'm here to protect the place from the riffraff and here you are."

I always wondered how a guy with missing teeth could eat his food, and I supposed now was not the right time to ask. He didn't look that smart. If we kept him talking, maybe we'd get out of here in one piece.

"Calm down," I said. "Tucker Davis, the lawyer, asked us to stop by and check on the property. When we found the back door ajar, we decided to check it out. As you can see, we're not here to steal anything."

"I never killed anyone before. It might be fun. Dump your bodies in the abandoned well out back where no one will ever find you."

His creepy laugh ran up my spine. "You're going to shoot us with a rental cop at the end of the driveway? He'll hear the shots, Einstein."

"She doesn't like problems. She'd want me to kill you."

"Who's 'she?'" I asked.

He ignored me, cleared his throat, and let the contents fly across the room.

"Let's deal," Fab said. "I have a key to the safe. It's yours if you let us leave." She held out her arm sideways. "No sudden moves, I'm taking the key out of my pocket, nice and slow."

Fab distracted him, kicking the gun out of his hand; it flew and landed across the room. She lodged her foot in his gut and he screamed, dropping into a heap on to the floor. I cracked him over the head with the handle of my Glock.

"Now what?" I asked. "Do you suppose 'she' is

the childlike Violet and wants moron here to kill people?"

Fab lifted his wallet off the bedside table. She took out the driver's license. "Says here, 'Gary Greene.' We'll tie him up and let it be Violet's problem, or whomever's."

"Where's the gun safe?" I asked, now knowing why we were here sneaking around. At least it's not pitch dark out. Fab had a preference for sneaking around late at night.

"Ivers was a cagey old guy. There's a fake wall in the garage and the safe is behind there. Only two people know that, and one is a dead guy. Wonder why he gave what's probably a pricey collection to me?"

I spotted a tie rack inside the open closet door, helped myself to three nice striped ones, and tossed one to Fab. I jerked Moron's legs together and wrapped the ties around his ankles, tying the ends in a knot. "Should we gag him?"

"No one would hear him screaming unless they were inside the house." Fab kicked him in the ass and retrieved his gun, using a stained pillowcase.

"I thought we'd get more information out of Gary here, before you kicked the crap out of him."

"Let's get the hell out of here. I'm hungry."

* * *

Fab pulled into the driveway. Home at last! "This can't be good news." I drew my Glock as a scruffy-looking man dressed in jeans and a naked woman T-shirt, sunglasses, and in desperate need of a shave, strolled away from the front door and stared. "Recognize him?"

Fab cut the engine, jerking her Walther from the back of her waistband. "On three, shoot. If he lives, we'll ask him what he wants."

"Let's try a little patience and ask first." She rolled her eyes at me. "Okay, we'll talk at gunpoint. Whoever shoots him first has to deal with the cleaner dude."

Despite the fact the man looked homeless, when he realized we weren't jumping out to greet him, he started in our direction full of arrogance and cockiness.

"I'll bet he's packing behind his back, jeans are too tight to be anywhere else," I said, noticing his muscled thighs. He wore his jeans well.

"Roll down the window," Fab instructed. "I'll show off my gun, you chat it up. But if he makes a sudden move, he's dead."

His eyes smoldered with anger, but his hands went straight in the air. "Hey, Madison, I'm a friend of Creole's."

"He looks like a friend of Creole's," Fab said.

"Or Didier if he hadn't bathed," I hissed and hung my head out the window. "Prove it."

"I have a badge in my left front pocket. I'll take it out slow." He eased his police badge out of his pants, demonstrating he had plenty of practice.

Fab and I got out. "I won't shoot you, but she will, in case that badge came from a costume shop. What do you want?" I asked.

"Creole's out of touch. Sent me here to let you know if you need anything to call, and I'll send a posse or show up myself."

"Why should I believe you? Your name?"

155

"Help," he said, and laughed at his own joke. "Creole said to tell you he's looking forward to dinner."

I reholstered my Glock. "You have a business card?"

"Give me your phone." He held his hand out. "Creole also said he'll be mad if he hears there's been another shootout in your backyard and you didn't call." Help couldn't take his eyes off Fab.

Fab glared at him. "You're lucky my boyfriend isn't here. He shot the last guy who was mean to me."

"Creole so owes me," he mumbled and handed me back my phone. He withdrew his phone, stopped the ringing. "I got you here under 'Crazy' so I'll know who's calling."

Chapter 24

"Get off your ass and let's go? Is that anyway to speak to your partner?" Fab fumed. She didn't care about the scenic route, only the shortest. She'd make The Cottages in record time.

"Didier laughed," I said, pulling my seatbelt tight.

"He and I will be having a talk about that later," she sniffed.

"How is life with your beautiful boyfriend?" I asked. Having met her ex-husband, she seemed to have broken the pattern of choosing psychos.

"He's the easiest to get along with ever, as long as I follow the rules."

"What are the rules?" I wanted to laugh. Fab never thought that rules applied to her.

In the distance, traffic stacked up at the signal, so she cut a driver off and zoomed through the alley. If she drove fast enough, she'd make the intersection before it turned green again.

"Thank goodness there are only two or I'd forget. Do what he tells me and don't get hurt."

"How are you doing with rule number one?"

"There are perks to being very naughty." She got a dreamy look on her face.

Didier really did get her, he was easy to get along with, and he cooked breakfast. He never created any chaos; quite the opposite, he had a way of calming

157

everything down, especially the women in the family. I appreciated that he looked for ways to make me laugh, to bring me out of the grumpiest of moods.

I peeked through half-squinted eyes. Not having heard a string of bad words, I assumed we made the light and it was safe to look again.

"What kind of ridiculousness is going on here today?" Fab asked parking in front of the office.

"Catch-up meeting and then I have a case of my own to investigate. For which you will graciously offer your skills, for free."

A car drove up and Kathy got out with a sack of groceries, waving to some ratty-looking guy behind the wheel. She looked surprised to see me and not very happy. Before I could say anything, she said, "I need a few more days on your money, my bank is investigating the check before issuing a refund. With moving and everything, I just don't have the cash. I'm sure you understand."

Out of the corner of my eye I saw her husband Ron come out the front door. Spotting us in the driveway, he turned and went back inside. "The cottage is paid for until the end of the month. If you can't get your money issues straightened out, move."

"I'll do my best," she sniffed. She favored the slutty look; the black G-string under her sheer beach skirt showed off her butt cheeks and not in a flattering way. A low-cut top revealed ample cleavage.

A loud whistle caught my attention and I turned. Mac stood at the pool gate waving her arm and holding the gate open.

"Mac's weirder than usual," Fab whispered.

How can that be?

Mac stretched out in a chair in hiked up, baggy purple shorts and a tank top, her lit-up tennis shoe-clad feet stretched out in front of her. She looked over her sunglasses at me. "I really did check those two out."

"Kathy doesn't know this yet, but one way or the other, they are out of here by the end of the month," I said.

Fab dragged a chair next to the fence, keeping one eye on the property. "I'll evict them." She pulled out her Walther, stroking it as she would with my cat, Jazz. "And no charge, you'll just 'owe me' for the rest of your life."

Mac laughed. "I got to work at dawn. Kathy and some bleary-eyed guy were having an argument, but she'd already cleaned the pool area and a garbage bag sat by the gate. They took one look at me and practically ran. There were at least four cars in the driveway and a few minutes later they left."

"Any good news?" I kicked off my shoes and put my feet in the pool.

"I saved the best for last," Mac said. "Apple and Angie left town, they said their good-byes when they got their checks earlier."

"I'm not washing cars," Fab said.

"It's going back to all automatic." I looked at her. "Where did they go?"

"Angie fell in love with a homeless pimp. He got them all bus tickets to the good life in Tampa. Angie's going to strip at some classy joint called the 'The Pole,' and he got Apple a job washing dishes at a pancake house."

"I'm not often rendered speechless. I don't know what to say," I said.

"Oh, I do," Fab said. "Good riddance."

"Do you know Kathy's schedule?" I asked Mac. "Next time she has a day off work let me know."

"When you pulled into the driveway," Mac said, "Joseph took Svetlana inside and slammed the door. He's mad because he doesn't want to rat on his neighbors. He's sided with Kathy since she brings him dinner every night."

"Next time we do one of these meetings, we need food," I said, standing up and waving to Mac.

I held out my hand to Fab. "Keys, please. Before you complain, you need to get out in a few blocks and snoop around a construction site."

"What am I finding out?"

"Is the house that the contractors are working on actually owned by Kathy and Ron? If so, when is the move-in date? Find out what you can. Take your phone, just in case."

* * *

"Thanks for the heads-up," Fab complained, climbing into the driver seat. "Ron and Kathy came in the front door. I heard her voice and slipped out the back."

"They didn't come up in a car." I parked halfway down the block in the driveway of a triplex and there had been no traffic.

"The construction company is actually owned by Ron's father who drinks every afternoon at Pete's Tavern. Ron is only an employee. I asked who the owner of the house was and the guy couldn't remember the client's name and it's not the Stones. Every once in a while, a BMW shows up, three people get out and walk around, inspecting the job, never say a word, and leave."

"Let's go to the big yellow house on Gulf Boulevard across from the Beer Garden. They just sold that house, plenty of time for the new owner to have moved in."

A few minutes later, we drove past their previous residence.

"That's interesting." I pointed to the big For Rent sign in the front yard, from a big-time rental agency. I called the number on the sign.

"Give me the phone," Fab said, and asked for Donna. After a pause, she said, "What do you know about Kathy and Ron Stone?"

Donna talked non-stop for a couple of minutes and Fab hung up. "They never owned the house. They were dead-beat renters who got evicted. She told me Kathy has anger control issues when she's not on medication."

"How do you feel about staking out The Cottages at midnight?"

Chapter 25

"Why are you driving the speed limit?" I asked.

"When we get to the curve, look left and you'll see a sheriff's car parked. He's there almost every night. Writes a fair amount of tickets," Fab said.

It surprised me that she ever drove slowly enough to catch a speed trap. We didn't make it to the curve when the sheriff flew out of his hiding spot, lights flashing, hot on the trail of a sports car flying down the Overseas.

"What's Didier going to say when he finds out you snuck out of the house in the middle of the night?"

"I didn't sneak anywhere. I told Didier exactly what we're doing. And also that since stake-outs are mind numbingly boring, we wouldn't be gone long."

"I only feel a little guilty dragging you away from your warm bed."

Fab laughed. "I told him no guns and no dead people, so let's try and keep my promise."

"Explain to me how a person can party every night, all night long, and manage to get to jobs and run a business? Some of Kathy's guests pass out by the pool; it's all fun until one of them drowns. And not one guest or tenant has called to complain and she has thus far managed to stay off the sheriff's radar."

"How would you get the pool cleaned? Does a body stink in the water?" Fab asked.

"Call that creepy crime scene cleaner friend of

Kevin's. Once the floater is fished out of the pool, he can come over and work cleaner magic. His business card says he can get stains out of almost anything."

"Have you been to Kathy's store?" Fab asked.

"I'll wait until she's sunning her overly-tanned body by the pool and go find out how much fun she is to work for."

"I smell drugs," Fab said. We knuckle bumped. "Great minds. You got a plan or do I need to throw one together in the next minute?" She turned the corner to The Cottages.

"Circle the block and park on a side street, we'll sit on the porch of the rental house across the street. The previous tenants didn't steal the patio chairs."

Fab parked on the opposite corner so that we could keep an eye on the Hummer. This wasn't a high crime area, but auto theft went in cycles and was on the rise again along with the occasional burglary. The thieves broke in when no one was home; they didn't want to get hurt, they just wanted to steal the good stuff and head straight for the pawn shop. We walked down the street, sticking close to the bushes, not a single light on.

"How long are we stuck here?" Fab fidgeted in her chair.

"An hour, we should have a pretty good idea what's going on. Then you can sneak back to bed."

"Thank goodness Didier is not an overprotective ass. This is the first relationship I've had where I don't screw with the truth. I lied to him once at the beginning and it almost ended us before we got started."

I had a vague relationship with the truth when it came to Zach—always with the good intention of not wanting to start a fight—and that had been a constant irritant. "I don't believe in the boogey man but I'm glad I didn't do this by myself."

"These are crappy chairs but it beats the ground," Fab said. She tipped the chair, hoping to dislodge the dirt. "Are you sure it's empty?"

"I know everything that happens on this block, except for my own property."

"Let me guess, you know all the neighbors names and their complete life history?"

"If you'd put on your happy face once in a while, people would talk to you too," I told her.

"No, thanks. Party time," she said and pointed.

Five people emerged from Kathy's cottage and piled into the cars; three backed out and two of them went in opposite directions, the third pulling back in. A pickup truck cruised around the corner and pulled in alongside.

"Who knew you could cram eight cars in the driveway? Good thing code enforcement doesn't drive by at night. Will you check out the pool area, since I'd be recognized in a second?" I pulled the Glock from my thigh holster. "Just in case."

Fab pulled her Walther, repositioning it in the back waist of her jeans.

"Try not to shoot anyone," I said.

"I'm more in the mood to kick someone's ass. Keeps me from getting rusty."

I knew no one would see me. There were no lights on this side of the street and no moon. Right before Twizzle died he got drunk, and when a few friends cheered him on, he shot the street lights out. By the time the sheriff arrived, everyone had scattered, leaving piles of broken glass every few feet. I called the city to find out where we were on the list for new light bulbs and had been told tersely, "At the bottom."

My eyes continuously darted up and down the street and I caught Fab's movements when she came around the side of the office between the bushes and ran back across the street.

"That was fast," I said.

"You need to get out the chlorine. A couple is doing it on the top step of the pool and another are getting started in one of the chaise lounges. There are remnants of a barbeque, piles of beer bottles, and cigarette butts everywhere. Apparently they haven't heard about ashtrays and threw trash all over the ground." Fab laughed. "The best part is, Joseph had his face pasted to the window, and was so glued to the sex action that if there hadn't been a screen, he'd have fallen out."

"If he's only watching, does that qualify as cheating on Svetlana?"

"Next time someone tells me I'm crazy, I'm going to tell them, 'Wait, meet my friend, I bet you'll change your mind.'"

"Five dollars you never get anyone to change their mind," I said.

"Guess who just turned the corner?" Fab pointed. "Just as two of our little partiers back out."

The sheriff car's lights went on and screeched to a halt in front of where we sat. Officer Johnson got out of the car, pointing his flashlight in our faces. We got off on the wrong foot when he transferred to the local sheriff's office, a case of instant dislike. He figured no one rents to criminals and is squeaky clean.

"This ought to be interesting," Fab whispered.

"Hands up where I can see them," Johnson ordered.

We both stuck our hands in the air. "Surely you remember me, Madison Westin." To my credit, I managed to sound respectful. "I own The Cottages across the street."

"Public records show that you don't own this property, so that makes it trespassing. Do you have a good reason for sitting here, or do I haul you in and let you explain it to a judge?"

The remaining cars left the driveway.

"I'm just doing what you asked, trying to keep nuisance calls to a minimum. I come by from time to time at night, to check and make sure all is quiet," I said.

Johnson shone his light in Fab's face. "And you have a criminal record a mile long."

"You must have me confused with someone else. I don't so much as have a ticket for jaywalking. If you need a reference, call Detective Harder, Miami police department." An ordinary citizen would have felt her foot in his smaller friend.

"Let's have a walk around your property," Johnson said, scanning every inch with his flashlight.

"That won't be necessary since all the party goers just left, just a few friends who got together for a barbeque," I said.

"I'm writing you both a citation. You don't get to use other people's property for whatever excuse you concoct. Get out your identification," Johnson ordered.

"If you call the owner, they'll verify they know me and have no objection to my sitting on their porch," I said. Mac had signed up to be property manager, but they hadn't sent back a signed contract. "Our IDs are in my SUV."

"It's the law that you're not supposed to be without identification. Don't move or I'll arrest you." Johnson went back to his patrol car.

"I've had enough of him," I hissed. "I've never done jack to that man."

"While you were engaged with that moron, Kathy came out, crept around cottage two, and tried to listen from behind the palm trees. She didn't stay long. After shifting positions a few times, she went back to her place, got a black garbage bag, and headed in the direction of the pool. Minutes later, she came back, handed the bag off to some kid young enough to be her grandson, he took it and disappeared between the front cottages and out onto the beach."

"I wonder if she knows it's me?" I asked. "Maybe I can get some good info out of Joseph in the morning."

"This could be worse," Fab continued to whisper. "Johnson could figure out we're armed and our concealed carry permits are also in the SUV."

"I'm sorry you got dragged into this because of me. I'll get us a lawyer to get the charges dropped."

"I have no doubt," Fab chuckled.

Johnson came back, ticket book in hand. "Sign here," he said, and pointed.

I signed and handed the book to Fab. "A heads-up, we'll both be in court with our lawyers, so you might want to schedule time off."

"You should be thanking me, instead of copping a pissy attitude. You could both be on your way to the

167

county jail."

Fab pinched my arm and I managed to keep my mouth shut. Johnson's eyes followed us as we walked to the corner. He sat at the stop sign and waited until we got in the Hummer, and followed us out to the main highway before turning in the opposite direction.

"Do you suppose he thought we were going to double-back?" Fab asked.

"We're not doing this again. I'll bribe Shirl and pitch it to her as though stake-outs are fun and adventurous. Or better yet, have you order her to do it." I laughed. "Mac would tell you to go screw yourself after blowing one of her gigantic bubbles, but not Shirl."

"You're a terrible friend."

Chapter 26

A perfect day dawned in the Keys, sun shining, birds chirping, when Fab and I pulled into The Wild Bird Farm, a dozen cars already parked around the large lot. We stopped at the house first and exchanged hugs with Tolbert. Since every room swarmed with helpful people, we snuck back outside. We boarded the church bus early, no reason not to get a good seat. No matter which one you chose, they were dreadfully uncomfortable. I shifted around unsuccessfully, each way I turned the edges of a spring poked me hard in the butt. This morning, I thought briefly about thinking up a good excuse as to why I couldn't attend Gus Ivers' memorial—we only had a brief business relationship, after all. No one else in town would take on the job of evicting road kill entrepreneurs. Then to my shock he mentioned me in his will, gifting me the whole block, which I still don't understand. Neither did his daughter, Violet, who I noticed hadn't shown up for her father's final hurrah.

I punched Fab's leg. "Get your feet off the back of the seat." We scored the back bench and spread out to discourage anyone from sitting down next to one of us. "Spoon needs to find someone to work a miracle and recover these seats and make them comfortable." He owned an auto body shop down by the docks. People whispered that illegal activities happened behind the barbed-wired fencing, but I'd never heard his name and law enforcement mentioned in the same sentence.

She growled, "Let's get out of here."

"You tell Tolbert we're leaving." I knew she'd never disappoint Tolbert and wipe the smirky smile of pleasure he got when he saw her come through the kitchen door. This would be his first opportunity to share doing what he loved with her. If he had his way, the both of us would attend every Sunday.

"Reminds me of high school when I'd sit in the back of the class with the bad boys, the criminals in training." I laughed. "You know they always tolerated my total adoration, but by today's standards I'd be labeled a nerdy girl."

"And here you are with a bad girl." She elbowed me. "There were no bad girls in my all-girl Catholic school. You either behaved or suffered the painful wrath of the nuns and their steel rulers. Did any of your classmates become real criminals?"

"All of them eventually turned into upstanding citizens with the exception of one, Barlass, and I don't know what happened to him. One day he didn't show up to school, so I asked around and found out his parents sent him to military school, which broke my heart since I'd had a huge crush."

The seats started to fill up. More than a few guests showed up who could be labeled riffraff, which surprised me due to Ivers' total lack of disdain for them. Free food couldn't have been the motive; that would be served after the service and attendance wasn't a requirement. Fab and I had picked up platters of sandwiches at The Bakery Café. We wouldn't lie and say they were homemade, but we

170

wouldn't correct anyone who wanted to think so.

Fab jerked on my arm. "Scooch down in your seat and maybe he won't see us."

Harder boarded the bus and stood by the driver's seat. He was Fab's least favorite detective. Today, he'd left his tight-ass look at home. This was one of the few times I'd seen him do normal—he'd be perfectly at home in a beach bar with his tropical shirt and shorts. All he needed was a drink in his hand. I knew he and Tolbert were friends, but had no idea he even knew Ivers.

The bus filled up quickly. I waved and motioned Harder to come and sit in the back with us. Tolbert stood in the front and welcomed everyone. Once full, he closed the bus doors and took the driver's seat.

Fab hissed, "I hate you."

I jerked her sleeve. "You put on your party manners," I hissed back, "or I'll tell Didier you embarrassed me after I begged you not to." I dabbed at my dry eye.

"He'd never believe you over me."

"Only if you lied to him." I wanted to laugh because I had her now and she'd never do that.

"Are you here to arrest anyone?" I asked when Harder sat down next to me. We had room for one more person, so I gave Fab a shove with my hips.

He shot a dog-smile at Fab. "My favorite criminal, and her sidekick. When this is over I have a few questions for you. I'd ask her"—he indicated Fab—"but she lies all the time."

"You two need to kiss and make up or something. I bet if you ask her nicely, she might cooperate with you once in a while," I said.

Fab crossed her arms and looked out the open window, as a cool breeze blew down the aisle.

"Did you know Gus?" I leaned into Harder so that he could hear me. "Or did you wake up this morning and say, 'I think I'll go to the memorial of someone I don't know.'"

His eyes narrowed and he ignored the question. "Have you seen Violet Ivers?"

I shook my head and wondered about his putting in an appearance. We rode along in silence until we pulled into Long Key Park, where everyone filed off and filled the picnic tables. Tolbert stood in the middle, holding up his hands, stopping all conversation. He looked at everyone and smiled. "We are gathered here today to remember and celebrate the life of Gus Ivers. It will be a short service, then we'll go around the table and everyone can express their thoughts." He pointed to a plumpish woman. "You're up, Polly."

Polly, middle-aged with long black hair, had been sitting in the front. She stood, clasping her hands, and belted out *Amazing Grace*. She had a set of pipes and clearly enjoyed her music. She followed with another song I didn't recognize but the woman could sing.

Now Tolbert's turn, he got up and started his eulogy. From the corner of my eye, I saw Harder retrieve a small note pad from his shirt pocket and jot down notes. I shifted closer so I could see and he poked me in the arm. I gave him a dirty look, leaned over farther, and noticed he'd written down names of people, or descriptions when he didn't know the person.

He flipped the page and wrote, *You're nosey*.

I counted the names on the page and matched

them to the person and seat. I pulled on his pen taking it from him and wrote names next to a few of the descriptions. Between the two of us we ID'd everyone. I supplied all the names of the lesser-known criminals. The mourners fell into two categories: well-known pillars of the community and the general riffraff. I'd say it ran 50/50.

One after the other, each person stood and gave us a glimpse into the life of the man. We found out he shot one guy in the butt for trespassing, then drug him to the hospital and paid the bill. He cheated at poker when he thought no one was looking. His favorite watering hole turned out to be The Croc, where locals hung out and discreet sex acts were performed right at the bar. He gave generously to charity and no one had an unkind word to say. He didn't loan or give money to fools which he'd tell you to your face, but he'd buy you a meal.

Not everyone spoke, and I planned to be in that group until Fab almost nudged me off the bench. I stood briefly and said, "Gus and I met through mutual business interests and I enjoyed our friendship." It sounded lame, but the truth was I hadn't known him long and we only had the car wash in common. It had pleased me that he never complained, probably because it made more of a profit than when he had full control. It would make more money than automated if I could find two new girls to wash cars half naked.

To my shock, Fab stood up. "I only knew Gus Ivers a short amount of time but I liked him. We got one another. He had a great dry sense of humor and was an outrageous flirt."

I glared at Harder, daring him to get up and say

something, but he just glared back and stayed seated. When everyone who wanted to had spoken, Polly stood and sang *Time to Say Good-bye*.

On the drive back to the farm everyone sat quietly at first, but when the first person broke the silence everyone started talking at once, and then the return trip seemed to go faster. The three of us stayed seated as everyone piled off the bus and over to the house. Fab stood and pushed by me. "You can fill me in later," she said, and started up the aisle.

Harder's jaw clenched. He wanted to talk to Fab and she was doing her usual cut and run on him, only the threat of jail had gotten her to stick around in the past.

"I don't mind that you leave Fab," I said sweetly, "but I won't share one word of information with you."

From the look on her face, I think she seriously entertained shooting me. I ignored her and turned to Harder. "You have questions for me?"

"What do you know about Violet Ivers?" he asked.

"Never met her before the reading of the will. She pitched a fit when she found out her father left bequests to other people. Of course, your friend, Tucker, is contesting." I noticed Fab hadn't left, sitting about three rows up. "I do know she's trying to sell off his gun collection."

"Have you been to her house, invited or otherwise?" he asked.

"No to either. But if you continue down this road, I'll need to consult my attorney."

"So that means you've been to Gus's house." He fixed me with his sneaky smile. "You've got Creole immunity; you'd have to kill someone to trump that. I'm not so worried he'd kick the crap out of me, which he'd do, I'm more worried that he'd leave the department and he's the best detective I've ever had, so if you keep it at the misdemeanor level I can overlook it."

He stood and fished his phone out of his pocket, scrolling the screen. "Do you know this guy?"

"Nice mug shot. He seems pretty proud to be getting his picture taken, strung out, hair sticking on end." I took his phone and showed Fab. "Gary Greene is his name. Flopping right now at Gus Ivers' house."

"Now isn't that an interesting piece of news. I'd like to talk to him, ask a few questions. He seems to have disappeared."

Fab snorted. "Whatever happened, we had nothing to do with it."

"The immunity you spoke of, does it extend to my friend here?" I asked Harder. When I could see that he salivated over the thought of arresting Fab, I added, "I'm sure the Creole deal you spoke of would include her."

"I feel sorry for Creole. You're going to drive him crazy." The corners of his mouth flickered up. "Agreed, her too," he said and pointed.

"We stopped by Ivers' place to check on the house, and we ran into Gary who was making himself at home in one of the bedrooms. He kept mumbling about a 'she,' and I assumed he was talking about Violet, since it's her house now."

"So you know him then." Harder mulled that over.

Fab, exasperated, said, "Kicking the crap out of him doesn't mean we know him."

"He pulled a gun but wasn't going to be satisfied

with just shooting us, he had big plans to cut us up and dump our bodies. Mentioned that 'she' wouldn't be happy if he let us live," I said.

"You're alive and now he's nowhere to be found, so how did your little visit end?" he asked.

"Fab kicked the gun out of his hand, I hit him over the head, we tied him up, and left."

"You still have his gun?" Harder asked.

I turned to Fab. "Do we?"

"You can have it," she fumed.

"And since we're being so cooperative, I see no reason to mention any of this to Creole. I'm not interested in one of his lectures where he growls through the whole thing."

Harder threw his head back and laughed. "I'm familiar with that voice."

"What did the coroner deem to be Ivers' cause of death?" I asked.

"Acute liver failure."

"That's odd. Ivers had recently gotten a clean bill of health from his doctor. You'd think a failing liver would get the attention of even a crappy doctor. Does Tolbert know?" Fab asked.

Harder nodded that he'd told Tolbert the disturbing news. "Let's go get some food before it's all gone."

Fab whispered, "Let's eat fast and get out of here. We can come back when everyone's gone home."

Chapter 27

I slept lousy and walked into the kitchen to find Fab and Didier all tangled up enjoying their coffee, which only annoyed me. Kissing and cuddling all the damn time only happened in books, not real life. Thank goodness the only thing that stood in the way of me and my coffee was the microwave.

"Didier, she was really mean to me yesterday." Fab pointed her finger and sulked. She turned her face slightly and smirked at me.

She should've waited for this nonsense until I drank my entire cup of coffee. "You want to see mean?" I exploded, coming around the island.

Didier stepped between us and held each of us by the arm. "As delightful as it would be to see the two of you roll around on the floor, it will not happen."

I jerked my arm away and yelled at Fab, "I can't believe you!"

She smiled at me and flipped her hair.

Just you wait, I silently mouthed to her. I gave Fab a phony smile and picked up my phone. "Saying something nice to me would motivate me to help make your legal problem go away."

Fab glared. "Okay, fine. Thanks or something."

Didier turned her face to his and frowned, which made me happy. "I'll tell you later," she told him. "It's a ticket and all her fault."

I called Cruz's office. Susie, his personal pit bull, answered the phone. She had been frosty to me ever since I cornered her boss at the courthouse without her permission. I had violated protocol; everything went through her first and then she decided if it was deemed worthy of Cruz's attention.

"Hi, Susie, this is Madison Westin. I have a legal problem to discuss with your boss." I hit the speaker button and put a finger to my lips.

"Don't you always," Susie mumbled. "Mr. Campion is not in. Give me the basics, so he'll have the information when he calls you back."

"Fab and I got a ticket for trespassing and we need a lawyer for our upcoming court date."

Dead silence. I assumed she hung up on me.

"You're calling one of the best criminal lawyers in this state for a trespassing ticket?" Her voice rose with each word. "Mr. Campion wouldn't let me bill you enough for wasting his time like that."

"Are you suggesting that I find another attorney?"

"I'm suggesting that you show up in court and handle it yourself. It's trespassing," Susie enunciated. "Worst case: a fine. My guess is you're guilty."

"It's not that simple," I started.

"It never is with you."

"Tell Mr. Campion that I'm looking forward to his aunt and uncle's return visit and if he has any additional requests, I'm sure he'll have you call me." If she didn't hate me before, she did now with my subtle attempt at blackmail.

"I'll let him know you called." Susie hung up on me.

"I'm surprised she didn't bang the receiver on the desk before she hung up. You can do that with business phones," Fab said.

"I'm calling the owners of the house and getting a notarized statement that we weren't trespassing. Mac has tentatively agreed to manage their two properties, just waiting to hear back."

"What's wrong with current management? They must have some as they live in one of those states that never see sunshine. How much sense does it make to own houses in Florida and live in below-zero weather?" Fab asked.

"Current management has no customer service. They're retiring in a couple of years and then we'll be neighbors." I wiggled my fingers. "Where are my keys?"

"Where are you going?" Fab tossed them to me.

"I have plans." I smiled and banged the front door closed before she could ask any more questions.

* * *

I zipped into the space in front of The Cottages' office. So I didn't have plans, but lovey-dovey got on my nerves.

Mac opened the door, looking pale. "We need to talk before the sheriff gets here," she said, and motioned me inside.

"You feel okay?" I shook my head. "What now? Let's sit out by the pool."

"Well, uh… you might want to sit down. I know I do." Mac pulled on a full skirt, covering up hot pink bicycle shorts, and threw herself back in her chair, propping her feet on one another. "You want to steer clear

179

of the pool. At least until they haul the dead chick out. Called you and it went to voicemail. My next call was to the sheriff. I got to work at the crack again this morning. I'm going home early and drink myself into a stupor."

I started to sit and changed my mind. "What do you mean, *dead?*"

"Hell if I know," she screeched. "I thought she'd passed out, beach towel over her head. I yelled at her to wake the hell up, and didn't get a twitch. I stomped over to kick the chaise, the towel dropped, didn't cover her entire face, and noticed she'd turned this weird bluish color and one eye looked half open. I screamed and ran back inside the office, calling Shirl; she told me what to do."

I paced back and forth in front of the window, my stomach churning, now happy I hadn't eaten breakfast. "Do we know her?"

"Never saw her before." Mac twisted her skirt in her hands.

"I'd better call Cruz. A dead body should get me to the head of the line." It surprised me when someone other than Susie answered, that had never happened before. I explained the problem and Cruz picked up immediately.

"Did you shoot this one?"

I relayed verbatim everything Mac told me. "Two sheriff cars just pulled into the driveway. What do we say?"

"Stick to the usual yes and no answers. If you get cuffed, call back." He hung up.

"Let's move this meeting to the barbeque area so that we can see what's going on," I said.

Mac started, "You need to send Spoon over here and have him tell Kathy and Ron it's moving time, and the sooner the better."

The first thing I noticed, that once again the beach chairs were missing. I knew better, which is why I only sprung for the cheap ones. Everyone in the neighborhood had a hard time hanging on to chairs sitting outside unless they were broken down. Recently, I'd found an old round wooden patio table at Junker's, a place I discovered while hiding out one night. The table was covered in chipped blue paint and now I'm currently on the hunt for some old Adirondack chairs, and the entire set would be chained down. Thank goodness I hadn't moved the old cement benches or we'd be sitting on the ground.

"Good idea. Without some major intimidation, I think they're here for the long run."

"Yesterday, I wasn't here long before Kathy pranced out carrying a trash bag in her bikini and some maid apron like you'd see as part of a Halloween costume. I'd already scoped out the pool area and found it to be littered with beer bottles, over-flowing ashtrays, and there were signs of crack use—a glass pipe, which I saw her shove in her pocket. In a separate bag she collected the copper Brillo, stems, lighters, you get the picture."

"It's clear to me that she's more than a partier," I said. "They have expensive habits and it takes money to do this every night. The Stones have to be dealing. Makes sense with all the late-night traffic." I shook my head. "I'll call Spoon. Maybe we should chain the pool gate at night until they move. All I need is for Sheriff Johnson to be the one to get the call to come out and investigate. He's threatened more than once, since that new law, to close down The Cottages."

Kevin explained it to me that if you, as a landlord, can't control your tenants from committing felonies, then the city would take you to court to wrest control of said property.

"Just thought you'd like to know Miss January's got a new drunk friend. This one's more her age, or at least the age she looks. They like to get on the Trolley and get off at random places, sit and drink vodka out of a brown bag, then forget how to get home."

Totally disgusted, I couldn't control myself and laughed. "So how did they get home?"

"Kevin saw them hanging out in a planter and gave them a ride. He said Miss January started crying, thought she was being arrested again. The other woman forgot where she lived and he brought them back here to sleep it off." Kevin's an all-around good guy and deserves a better partner than Johnson, who would've taken them to the drunk tank.

The coroner van rolled past us. Must be a slow day, they made it in record time. Two sheriffs approached, looking vaguely familiar; new recruits. One stayed back when his phone rang.

The one standing in front of me looked fresh from the police academy. "Miss Westin," he drawled, "did you know the deceased?"

"I arrived just ahead of you and didn't go to the pool area. My manager, Mac Lane," I said and nodded in her direction, "says no."

"My guess is that she'll be in the system," he said. "Looks like a drug overdose. When the neighborhood wakes up and starts talking, call me if anything would suggest otherwise." He handed me his business card and left.

"Did that seem too easy?" I asked. "Do you suppose we need the crime scene cleaner dude?"

"These guys can spot foul play in a hot second," Mac said. "My guess is we don't need cleaner dude, but I'll call his weird ass and run it by him. At the least, I'll get the entire area power washed and more chlorine in the pool," Mac said.

"How's Joseph doing?"

"He hangs inside with Svetlana too much. I think he needs to deflate her and find himself a real woman. But I'm afraid she'll be as bad as the last one he brought around." Mac looked behind me, licking her lips. "Damn he makes my knees weak."

"Joseph?" I turned in my chair and felt her smack my shoulder. Creole strode across the drive. He had me in his sights and was not looking happy. "Let's not bring up the dead body unless he does first," I whispered.

"Hello, ladies." He winked at Mac.

Mac let out a giggly sigh. "Always nice to look at you," she flirted.

He walked over and held out his hand, so I stood up. "Excuse us," he said to Mac, pulling me out of the far gate to the beach. "Where's your date?" he growled.

I looked at him. "Are you jealous?" One look and I knew teasing him was the wrong tactic. "I don't have a date, swear."

He wrapped his fingers in mine and we walked down to the water, the waves lapping our feet. "I just came from your house and Fab told me different. Both she and Didier were surprised that it wasn't with me and so am I, quite frankly."

"How does 'plans' translate to 'date'? And if you would have showed up and I did have a date, you'd do what?"

"Drag you away and lock you in a holding cell until my case is over." He swept me up and walked me backward onto the sand, where he sat down and pulled me onto his lap. "You need reminding about not dating?" Without waiting for an answer his lips clamped down on mine.

I pushed hard on his chest. "Stop, I can't think when you do that."

He chuckled in my ear. "Time's up, I'm out of patience, not waiting any longer. When I get back, I'm taking you somewhere with no interruptions and will unleash my charm until you come up with an answer I like."

I ran my fingers through his dark hair.

Why didn't I just tell him yes, damn it, yes? Fear. What-ifs. Mother.

"You'll be careful won't you?" I asked.

"Give me a reason," he whispered, his bluest of eyes devouring me.

I tangled my fingers in his hair, pulling his mouth to mine and putting everything I had into the kiss.

"That says yes to me." He kissed me again. "I have to go," he said, pushing me to my feet and putting his arm around me. "Walk me to my truck. I have time for one more kiss."

I held up my finger. "Just one?"

"You know I keep my word."

Chapter 28

Kathy's store, Beach Chic, was a typical souvenir store. Clothing, postcards, beach paraphernalia one could stuff in your travel bag as proof you had a great time on your vacation. I wandered over to the seashell aisle in case I ran into Kathy and had to purchase something. I spotted a salesclerk displaying bathing suits over next to the side window.

"Is Kathy in today?" I asked.

The young girl looked up, surprised. "She doesn't work here anymore. She got fired."

So much for being the owner. "For what?"

"We're not allowed to talk about her." The girl looked to the front, the other clerk busy with a customer.

I reached into my purse and pulled out a twenty, holding it out. "This will be our little secret. Why was she fired?"

She jerked the money from my fingers. "Kathy pertinear stole everything in the store. The boss treated her like kin, and is spitting mad. Thousands of dollars in inventory! Doesn't understand why or what she did with it all. I did notice she always wore the clothes off the rack but figured she paid for them."

"How long has she been gone?"

"A week. The police were here talking to the boss lady. That's why we're not supposed to talk."

"Anyone else come by asking about her?" I asked.

"A couple of her friends stopped by right after she got fired and then no one after. I really should get back to work."

As I walked back to my SUV it dawned on me that the reason Kathy always walked around with price tags attached to her clothes was that she must have an outlet for stolen goods other than the flea market, since she was always around weekends. Not out of the realm she had a fence specializing in stolen merchandise, weekend markets could be very lucrative along with garage sales that were extremely popular.

I sat in the parking lot thinking about what to do next. Kathy had her fingers in too many illegal pies and I didn't want them exploding on my property. My butt started to ring; I lifted slightly so I could answer.

"Hey, girlie. This is the professor. Why did you tear down the car wash?"

"What the heck are you babbling about? Have you been drinking?" *Where the hell is my aspirin?*

"I left early this morning, Clean Bubbles occupied its usual place on the corner, the only thing amiss was that the trash can had been overturned. Came home, and it's now a vacant lot. Just so you know I don't start drinking until late afternoon."

"That makes no sense. How does a business disappear in a few hours? I'll be right over."

* * *

I screeched around the corner to Clean Bubbles and sure enough, there was no sign that a business had ever been there. The property was completely cleared; not even a

186

speck of trash remained. I pulled over in front of the trailer court.

"Any idea what happened?" I asked the professor, trying not to scream. He didn't bother to put on his pants for this visit.

"The girls from Twinkie Princesses," he said, and pointed to the roach coach parked in front of the sidewalk, "said a bulldozer came by knocked it to shit and hauled away every last piece."

I hadn't actually met the Princesses since every time I drove by they had a Closed sign displayed. I heard that they specialized in fried food. Didn't matter what you might request, they'd at least try to fry it up for you. "Anyone get a name?"

"Nope. You have a boyfriend?" He twitched a smile and gave me a wink.

"As a matter of fact I do, and he wouldn't have an aversion to beating the hell out of a crazy old man."

"I'm in pretty good shape for an oldster." He flexed his biceps. "Keep me in mind, I like redheads."

I'm going home and getting drunk. I pushed speed dial for Kevin and said when he answered, "I need to report a crime or more like an incident."

"Another dead body?" he snorted.

"No dead people. Someone came out and bulldozed Clean Bubbles without my knowledge or permission. Isn't that a crime?"

"You're calling me about that damned car wash? Good, one less place for criminals to conduct their late night activities."

"That's not very helpful when we're kind of like family." I should be embarrassed to mention a non-existent relationship. Kevin and I had a few unpleasant verbal exchanges and after that, our tepid relationship went cool.

"If Liam didn't like you so much I'd hang up on you. Whoever bulldozed had to get a permit. Check with the city." He did hang up this time.

I thought about Gus Ivers and was relieved that I didn't have to be the one to tell him his first business had been demolished.

* * *

I called the city of Tarpon Cove to find out about any demolition permits for the car wash and got an overworked woman who had zero interest in my problem. She did finally say that she had nothing on file and if I had bulldozed it without permits, then the city would level a fine.

It hadn't taken long for Spoon to get back to me. He made a few calls and found out that Owen's Demo did the job, my name was on the invoice, and they were paid in cash. According to Owen, I had insisted at the time of the demo that I had the proper permits, which they didn't bother to verify. The fact that Owen overlooked little things like permits was why he'd gotten the job. Not to mention cash is king. The best part was that whoever impersonated me had red hair.

"I don't dare make an insurance claim. They'll want to put me in jail if they hear that story," I said.

Spoon also informed me he beat on the door at the Stones', and when they didn't answer he stuck his head in the open window and introduced himself, telling them to be out by the end of the week.

"Don't make me come back here." They got the message loud and clear, he assured me.

Chapter 29

Mac called, saying Shirl had called her all excited that The Cottages were surrounded by the sheriff's department and that they had gone door to door demanding everyone stay inside.

"What the hell is going on now?" Fab asked, rounding the corner and parking in the driveway across the street.

Sheriff's cars blocked The Cottages' driveway and they parked several more in the street. Kathy sported handcuffs and was being perp walked down the driveway, her head pushed slightly down to get her in the back seat of one of the patrol cars. At that moment, she thought it was a good idea to crack the sheriff in the chin with her head and try to make a run, but she got about a foot away before another officer tasered her, and she slumped to the ground twitching.

Johnson walked across the street. "Trespassing again? Leave now or this time I'll take you to jail."

"Mac Lane is the property manager and I have every right to be here," I told him.

"Can you prove that?" he sneered.

"I have my lawyer on speed dial if you'd like to confirm my story." I had so annoyed Cruz I'm not sure he'd pick up. "What happened?" I pointed to my property. When he didn't respond I asked, "Did you hear about the ticket? You won't have to schedule time off to go to court.

It got dismissed."

His face filled with fury. He turned away without a word and stomped back across the street.

"Cruz came through on our tickets?" Fab asked.

"More like Susie. She's right, Cruz would never appear on a misdemeanor ticket. Oh, and I'm sending you the bill."

It surprised me that the chairs were still on the front porch. We settled in with a bird's-eye view straight up The Cottages' driveway, we could see every bit of activity.

"What the hell for?"

"When Susie called back with the good news, she said Cruz told her to take a long weekend due to all the difficult clients she'd been dealing with, and suggested she lounge her butt in a waterfront cottage."

"And she had the nerve to ask for free?" Fab inspected her chair carefully, giving it a good bang on the post before sitting.

"I was a little disappointed in the nice girl routine. I'd have enjoyed some skilled blackmail. Hopefully while she's here no one gets arrested or shot, I want to save that for when Cruz's family comes to town, they enjoyed the drama the last time."

Fab took out her phone. "Get your asses over to the drug house and hurry up."

"I can't believe you abuse my employee or her friend like that. You'd better not need to go to the hospital, no perks for you." Both Mac and Shirl had girl crushes on Fab, and they were probably excited they got the call.

The two of them snuck up, dragging their beach

chairs between the palm trees that filled the small grassy area in front of the office.

"What in the hell is going on?" I asked.

"Finally, something good happens." Shirl snapped her chair open. "Apparently, the Stones have multiple felony warrants. His are chicken change in comparison to Kathy's." She pointed. "Oh, look! The dogs are here."

Two K-9 units rolled up. The back doors opened and the dogs jumped out, sniffed the tires, took a pee, and were ready for work.

"Glad I'm not Ron," Mac said. "Those two must have seen the sheriffs rocket into the driveway. Before they knocked, the neighbor told the cops Ron climbed out the bathroom window, jumped the fence, and sprinted down the beach."

Shirl laughed. "Joseph, with tears in his eyes, told me they were headed to a little hideaway in the Glades until everything died down. They might have made it, if they hadn't come back to loot the cottage of the furniture."

"Every damn time we rent to a lowlife, they take whatever is not nailed down before they leave," I said. Frankly, I tired long ago of replacing furniture, which didn't get stolen as often as the televisions and microwaves.

"Kathy put herself under the scrutiny of the Feds when she hooked up with a forger and started passing fraudulent cashier's checks. They take a dim view of ripping off banks. I also heard Beach Chic pressed charges for the stolen inventory," Mac said.

"How do you two get your information?" Fab asked.

"I know every sheriff on the force," Shirl said,

preening. "If you were friendlier, you'd have known this was going down ahead of time." She shook her finger at me.

I glared at her. "You're nervy."

"Almost forgot the best part." Mac unwrapped the paper off a lollipop and shoved it in the inside of her cheek. "Kathy was under investigation in the disappearance of her missing ex-husband and his girlfriend. That happy couple used to like to brawl until the cops showed up. He always wore the marks of having had the crap kicked out of him. More than once, they found him balled up and bleeding. Then he and his current girlfriend disappeared, no trace, his family screaming 'murder.'"

"None of this came up in a background check?" I narrowed my eyes at her.

"Fake last name for her. Ron's using his dead brother's name."

"Turns out Kathy won't fry for double murder. The ex thought it would be funny to stage an apparent death and skip town, not staying in touch with anyone. They got bored when she didn't get arrested and came back," Shirl said.

I covered my face, taking a breath, and looked at Shirl. "What else?"

"Kathy has multiple drug-selling charges in another county. Ron also has drug charges, selling, possession, and bench warrants in three counties. He doesn't like to appear in court."

I shook my head. "Remind me in the morning to take felons, pimps, and addicts off the welcome sign in front of The Cottages."

Shirl looked excited over her next piece of news. "The dead girl didn't die by the pool, her body had been moved. Same neighbor—the old man in the two-story—called the cops the next day when he heard the gossip about the girl and said he saw her stumble outside into the gravel next to the Stones' cottage and never got up. A few minutes later, two guys came out of Kathy's place, took hold of her hands and legs, and went into the pool area. Now we know how she ended up in the chaise."

"If the sheriff can prove that she died from drugs used inside their cottage, neither of them will get out of jail for a long time," I said. "Or worse, the Stones sold them to her."

Mac hit my arm. "Here comes Ron's parole officer."

"Evening, ladies," a basketball-player-tall black man said, looking like he'd had a long day in his rumpled suit. "I'm Ron Stone's PO, Alvin Black."

"We'd offer you a seat but we're out of crappy beach chairs." I made the introductions.

"Sorry for the inconvenience, but we'll be here until the dogs drag Stone back and then I can check his junky ass off my list. Next time I need to speak to him I won't have to go looking very far, he'll be sitting in a jail cell. Good thing we got here when we did, that so-called wife of Ron's would have led us on another chase through the swamps again. If that furniture belongs to you, I'm happy to add on another charge," he said.

"If I could get my furniture back tonight I wouldn't press charges, but if I have to wait until after a trial then go ahead," I said.

He laughed. "Been down this road before?"

"Pawn shop experience." I laughed back. "You might consider that they passed me a fraudulent cashier's check. My bank says despite what they say, no bank ever issued that check. The bank manager requested a meeting with Kathy, but she didn't show up and declined to speak with anyone. They did close her account," I related.

"And to think I stopped by to discuss a dirty drug test with Stone. I imagine Kathy knew if she showed up at the bank, she'd leave in cuffs."

"If we only had some popcorn," Shirl said.

The paramedic wagon turned the corner, lights flashing.

"They must've found Ron," I said. "You think he was stupid enough to fight off police dogs?"

Mac pointed. "They're dragging his ass across the driveway now." Ron, bent over at the waist, hands cuffed behind his back, struggled with the cops who had him under control. The paramedics met him with a stretcher, pulling the straps tight until he yelped. The lights along the drive and in the trees showed that Ron's shirt and pants had been torn and there was blood rolling down the side of his face. His arms and legs covered in sand and dirt, he looked like he'd been mauled by a pack of dogs instead of just two. The medics gave him a brief look-over and shoved him none-too-gently in the back of the EMS wagon and sped off.

Mr. Black walked back over, saying, "Get the truck unloaded before the tow truck gets here and you can keep your furniture."

"Leave the chairs here, we may need them again." I pulled on Fab's arm. "Come on, princess, you too."

"I don't like manual labor." She pouted.

I frowned. "That's so sad. If you don't help, I'll non-stop whine about it for the next week."

Mac and Shirl were glued; it wouldn't surprise me if they were rooting for Fab to tell me off.

Chapter 30

Fab and I had our feet on the railing, kicked back on the deck at Jake's. She just beat me soundly at pool, taking no mercy. I'm not sure why I subjected myself to the humiliation. It wouldn't surprise me if she'd hustled men out of cash at some time or another.

"No one died today?" Fab inclined her head toward the door.

"Be nice. I think this is their first time." I waved to Dickie and Raul.

The pair looked oddly out of place here at Jake's, Dickie in his wrinkled polyester pants and rolled up sleeves of his dress shirt and Raul in a shorts and a muscle shirt showing off his well-developed biceps. They slid into chairs opposite Fab and me.

Raul looked around. "A lot cleaner than when Jake owned the place."

"Come by for your free lunch?" Fab winked at Raul.

Dickie cleared his throat. "We need to hire the two of you for a little business problem."

I motioned the waitress to take their order; it's always easier to talk over food and drink. "We're happy to help, aren't we, Fab?" I nudged her leg.

"For you two, we'll do it for free." She smirked at me.

Fab bonded over board games with Raul during a

short stay at the funeral home. Her relationship with Dickie had improved; at least she didn't scare him anymore. I'd never let her forget she agreed to a freebie.

"Slow today?" I asked politely.

"We picked up two bodies this morning, their families will be in tomorrow," Dickie said. "One indicated they'd like a themed funeral." He sighed.

"I told him not to stress it. I got a referral to a quirky party planner up in Miami who thinks outside the box," Raul said, patting Dickie on the shoulder.

"Another word for weird crap." Fab laughed.

I bit my lip and tried to keep a respectful look on my face. "How can we help you?"

The waitress delivered our drink order.

"We hired a new guy, Butch, to help with transportation. He works the night shift. Problem is, he picks up bodies and then doesn't return for several hours. We know some of these trips should take less than an hour because most of them are local. We need to know what he's doing. What if it's something criminal and he brings bad publicity to Tropical Slumber? Scandal is not good in our business," Raul told us. "We've never had a single complaint."

"When does he work again?" Fab asked. "This should be easy enough to wrap up in one night."

Every time we think it's going to be an easy job we get shot at. How much trouble could a guy hauling dead bodies around get into?

"He starts work in a few hours. Even when he doesn't have pickups he's gone all night. He slips away with a reasonable excuse and is evasive upon return," Dickie said.

"We'll put a tracker under the Cadillac. It will make it easier for us to follow him and know where he is at all times. We'll head over now and wait for him. Let you know in the morning what he did with his time." Fab smiled at Raul.

* * *

"Not one word from you in the future about weird cases," I told Fab.

We parked at the tattoo parlor next door to the funeral home. The streets had little traffic, not that it would be hard to follow a hearse.

"Do you think Butch is stupid enough to take a hearse on a crime spree?"

"We've made the acquaintance of some really stupid people, so it's hard to say," I said.

"Party's on." Fab pointed to a small truck pulling in the driveway.

A twenty-something-year-old husky dude stood under the lights that illuminated the parking lot. Right on time, he disappeared inside the funeral home and came out about an hour later, slipping behind the wheel of the Cadillac.

"How are we going to remain inconspicuous when there are only two cars on the road—his and ours?" I asked. "Do not turn off the headlights."

"I already thought about that, but with our luck we'd get pulled over and given a ticket."

We followed him in the direction of The Cottages until he turned off the main highway into a residential neighborhood. We hung back and he pulled up in front of a small house. After circling the block, we sat at the corner. A few minutes later, a longhaired brunette came running out of the house and jumped into the passenger side.

"Let me guess, his girlfriend?" I asked.

Butch cut through an alley back to the main highway. He drove along the coast and pulled into the main beach parking lot and up to the sand and parked. The twosome got out and held hands, walking across the beach in the direction of the water.

"I want to go home," I whined. "How many nights are we going to have to follow him to figure out what he's doing?"

"We're going to wait. I'm not following them." Fab took a pair of binoculars from the console box. "Let's hope this is his idea of a date night and nothing more. I hate this job already. Why don't I threaten the truth out of them?"

"They're headed back already," I said. Butch had scooped the girl in his arms and spun her around. She wrapped her legs around his waist, clad in her bra, shirt in hand.

Five minutes later, the Cadillac hadn't moved.

I covered my face and laughed. "Bet you they're using it as their love shack."

"You're nasty. Nobody would do that. Dead bodies have been in there."

"I'm over this freebie of yours. I'm going to go peek in the window." I opened the door and grabbed a flashlight from the back.

"Wait up. I'm not missing out on this."

I crossed the parking lot and saw that neither of

them were in the front seat, unless they were laying or scrunched down. To make sure, I peered in the window. The only other choice made me shudder; they had to be in the back. I tried the door and found it locked so I beamed my high-powered flashlight through the windshield, moving it around.

Butch yelled, "What the hell?" He peered through the viewing window.

"Get your pants on and get the hell out here," I yelled, using my best growling mad voice.

Fab went around to the back, slipped her lock-pick out of her pocket, and threw open the doors. The couple was buck naked and scrambling to get into their clothes.

"You're not the police," Butch yelled.

"I never said I was. Impersonating a cop is a crime," I said. "We're private investigators." I wasn't, but he didn't need to know that I lacked a license. "Is this what you do every night, screw in the back of a hearse?"

"None of your business," he said.

"Do you have one of these?" Fab showed off her Beretta in her front waistband. "If not, answer the damn question. You're making me cranky and when that happens I get erratic."

The girl started crying. "I knew this was a bad idea." She glared at Butch.

"We're just having sex. We don't get a lot of private time," he said. "Satisfied?"

"What happens when you have a body here in the back?" I asked.

"We do it in the front," the girl sniffed. "There's not enough room with the casket."

201

Fab cleared her throat behind my back. If she laughed I would turn around and hit her. I had Mac run a background check on Butch before we arrived at the funeral home and he came back clean. My criminal antennae spoke to me that the girl didn't have a record either.

"Here's the deal. You tell Dickie and Raul when you get back what you've been doing. If they fire you, take it gracefully and hit the road. I hear of any problems and I'll have her kick your butt," I said, and pointed to Fab. "If she can't get the job done, just keep in mind I've been known to shoot people."

We turned and walked back to the SUV.

"Let's keep this job to ourselves," I said. "I'd rather find missing cats."

"Would you...?"

"No!"

Chapter 31

Fab and I lounged by the pool eating enchiladas from Jake's. Take-out was another cool perk of owning a bar.

Fab's phone rang and she looked at the screen with suspicion, but answered anyway. "It's pasty-faced Violet," she covered her phone and whispered, and then pushed the speaker button.

"Why aren't you returning Mr. Davis's phone calls?" Violet whined. "He's such an important man to have to keep making the same call over and over, not to mention the charge to the estate. He bills for every little thing."

I stuck my finger in my mouth. Loathing wasn't strong enough for how I felt about Tucker Davis, disreputable attorney-at-law.

"What do the two of you want?" Fab demanded.

"No need to be so surly," Violet said. "Daddy left envelopes for everyone and yours seems to be missing. Did you take it?"

I covered my mouth and laughed. Fab glared at me.

"How could I have done that? Tucker never handed them out and informed everyone he'd be hanging on to them until the estate is settled. Now he claims they're missing. They're probably in his desk drawer."

"Could you stop by Daddy's later? I'd like to hear more about your relationship with him, and I thought we'd come to a deal on the gun collection."

A grown woman whose voice sounded like that of a small child irritated me. I shook my head no at Fab. I never liked the woman; not that she gave me a reason to dislike her, but the hairs on my neck spoke to me.

"I'll stop by."

"I'm here at Daddy's now going through the heartbreaking task of cleaning everything," she sniffed.

After Fab hung up, I said, "Don't go. I don't trust her. Why make a deal on the gun collection when she's contesting the estate and the court could award her everything?"

"Of course I'm going. I want to see what she's offering." Fab patted her Walther.

"I'll call Didier," I threatened, knowing it was underhanded, but when he told her not to do something, she listened.

"You will not." She jerked my arm. "You're coming with me." She dragged me off my chaise and pushed me through the fence, a shortcut to the driveway.

"Why can't you meet her at a restaurant and do lunch?" I glared at her. "If we met at Tucker's, they at least have a snack bowl in the reception area."

Fab looked me up and down. "You need to cut back on the junk food."

"My Glock is loaded."

* * *

"Why are there no cars?" I asked. We pulled into the driveway of Gus Ivers' house, the guard no longer on duty. "It doesn't look like anyone's home."

"It will give us time to check the garage and make sure she didn't find the safe." Fab parked along the side of the house and slid from behind the wheel.

I hustled to catch up. "Was the garage door padlocked before?" I pointed to the overly large lock.

"There's a side door. She'll never know we were snooping around." Fab slid her lock pick from her pocket. She never left home without her tools of the trade.

Lying on top of a couple of garbage bags in front of the roll-up doors was Gary Greene crumpled in a very dead heap. My guess, it had something to do with the hole in the back of his head. He couldn't have been dead too long, as the inevitable stench wasn't evident.

"I think I'm going to be sick," I said.

"Go outside, stay out of sight, and call your friend Harder. Then we're getting the hell out of here."

I slipped around the corner of the garage where I had a view of the entire yard. Gary wasn't my first dead body, but it didn't get any easier. I wasn't sure how Dickie enjoyed his job so much. He always seemed happy to have another body to coif and dress.

Harder's phone went straight to voice mail, but I knew him to be obsessive about listening to messages. "You know how you were looking for Gary Greene? Well, he's dead in Ivers' garage. Send help when you get this. We're only about 50/50 at getting out of stupid situations."

Violet drove in and parked in front of the garage. I crouched behind an old outhouse, the purchase of which Gus had been proud of for those times his septic tank backed up. I'd used an outhouse once at a flea market and had almost fallen in the hole, so now I don't go within a foot of one. I wanted to ask Gus if he'd heard that Tarpon Cove had sewer lines and that he could hook in, but figured he'd never spend the money.

I stared opened-mouthed in disbelief as Violet and her male friend got out of the passenger side packing guns at their sides. Her makeover stunned me. She had ditched the Bo Peep look for tight skinny jeans and knee-high black leather boots. There was such a harsh glint in her eye I didn't think her whininess capable. I whipped my Glock out. From this vantage point I could shoot one or the other, which still left one to shoot Fab. I never had a clue that the little girl persona had all been an act.

Violet slipped her gun into her waistband, and she and her cohort put their heads together. Whatever they were discussing spelled big trouble for Fab and I. One dead, four with guns. Damn it.

She surveyed the property, then walked over and stuck her head in the garage. She ditched her whiney little girl voice to bark at Fab. "Come out, Miss Merceau, so we can come to terms."

Fab came out, Walther in hand.

"That's so unfriendly." Violet made a motion to put her hands in the air, and pulled her gun. "Throw yours on the ground. Two against one aren't good odds for you."

Fab looked her over from head to toe and dropped her gun; the makeover even shocked her.

"On your knees," Violet ordered. "Or I'll be forced to shoot you and I have something else in mind." She swept her hand out. "The nice thing about acreage is the neighbors never bother you and no one will hear your screams."

Fab gave her the finger and continued to stand her

ground. "What do you want?"

"You're going to die, but I think an overdose would be a much more fitting end to the whore who seduced my father." Violet laughed. "I'll need to get creative getting rid of your redheaded friend, can't have everyone dying the same way."

She'd given her delusional plans some thought. They sounded methodical and well-planned. There were no babbling signs of mental illness, but rather more like fury that there had been a hitch in her strategy.

"What happened to Gary in there?" Fab motioned to the garage with her head.

"He thought he could blackmail me."

"It's sad when you commit felonies with friends and they turn on you," Fab sniffed. "Blackmailers are never satisfied."

"I knew he wasn't bright but he thought I'd actually cave in to his demand. He'd already become a liability, but little did he know he just hastened his inevitable death."

"Violet you can tell me, what did Gary have on you?" Fab asked.

I admired the fact that Fab never flinched, even under threat of death.

"Idiot, his conscience started bothering him after I brought Daddy home in a nice urn. Interestingly, his shame came *after* the old man expired. Gary worked around here doing odd jobs, so it was very easy for him to spike Daddy's iced tea with anti-freeze. Did you know it's sweet and undetectable in a drink and brings about certain death?" She reached inside her pocket and took out a hypodermic needle, waving it at Fab.

And wouldn't you know it, my phone rang.

Violet and her friend turned, and I got off a shot in the confusion. Although I was aiming for Violet, her partner moved forward at the last second and I hit the guy in the shoulder. He fell backward, screaming. Violet was enraged. She took aim in my direction and pulled the trigger. Ready for return fire, I dropped down and ran for the row of trees and tall grass that Fab disappeared into after she beat a hasty retreat around the back of the garage. Hopefully, she wouldn't fall into the murky creek water.

"Oh, shut your mewling mouth," Violet yelled in the man's face. She raised her gun and shot him point blank.

I knew this was a bad idea. I hoped Harder would send help when I didn't answer his return call.

"Over here," Fab whispered. She had submersed herself into some varied types of swamp grass that grew five feet out of the knee-high water in which she stood.

"Did you happen to pick up your Walther?" I whispered back. "Or are we sharing one gun?"

"I never thought about the gun, I stayed focused on getting away from psycho without a bullet wound. Can you believe the transformation?" Fab asked, still shocked. "How did she manage to carry off two completely different personalities without anyone noticing?"

"My guess is that Gus and personality number two clashed and he wasn't impressed. That's probably the reason for the last-minute change up of his affairs." The last thing I wanted was to join her in the filthy water, but didn't see a different option. I squeezed my eyes closed for a minute, took a deep breath, and reached for her hand before wading into the crusty, slimy stream.

"I say we hide out here and make Violet come to us. We have no idea what's back that way." Fab motioned. "If it gets any swampier we could hook up with an alligator. I don't know what would be worse, being kibble for a gator or running into Violet."

"I don't hear anything. What does that mean?" I whispered. "I can't imagine her leaving. She can't let us live now. We know too much."

"We're in for the long haul. She needs to kill us but we're highly motivated to stay alive. Did you get a hold of Harder?"

I took my phone out. "He was the missed call." I pushed redial. The screen showed "dialing" and then it disconnected. After a third try, the call went straight to voicemail. "Help!" I whispered.

"Stop looking at me like that," Fab said. "I'm sorry. You were right, damn it."

"Why is it when we get in these situations one of us is always saying sorry?" I hissed.

A volley of shots rang through the air. "I know you bitches are in there," Violet snarled. "Come on out, I've got two automatics and extra ammo. I'll show that I can play nice. Tell me where the gun collection is and we can work a deal."

Fab and I looked at one another and shook our heads. Not saying a word, we stayed crouched in the grass. A not-so-dead gigantic Florida bug tried to latch itself onto my arm and I managed not to scream, but rather sent it skipping across the water with my other hand, scrubbing furiously with the slimy water. In order for Violet to find us, she'd have to jump in the water. Drowning her would be a pleasant option.

More shots rang out. "I know you can hear me, there's no escape. The only way out is through the fence, and there's no access through the swamp. Get out here now," she screeched, sounding frenzied, "or I'm going to spray this area with bullets. When one of you starts to bleed the buzzards will lead me right to you."

Fab had better getaway skills than I did, with years of practice before I met her, so I passed her my Glock and hoped to hell that she could get us out of here. I held up nine fingers to let her know how many rounds were left. Thank goodness I never went anywhere without a full clip. I did that once and had to listen to an intense lecture from Brad after showing up for target practice unprepared.

"Move," Fab said, and shoved me ahead of her. "She shoots, we crouch and crawl through the water. We're going to make her come to us, even up the odds. I'm conserving our bullets in case she finds us."

If the water got deep, Fab and I were good swimmers, even though the thought of lowering my body into the muddy, filthy water made me nauseous. We continued to slog through the grass as quietly as we could. The twigs and branches didn't make it easy, reaching out for bare skin and leaving long red scratch marks, not to mention that gnat season had begun and they were swarming. The miniscule bastards made a buzzing sound when they got close to my ear, taking a nip and leaving a burning sensation.

We caught our first break when the first wave of bullets whizzed through the trees, and we realized that she had gone in the opposite direction. She ripped off a couple more rounds and, judging by the gun fire, turned our way.

After a short trek, a break in the trees revealed the fence that straddled the property lines. The neighbor had cleared their acreage, leaving no cover for a good hiding place. We couldn't leave the security of the swamp since the only way out was over the six-foot chain-link fence, and we'd instantly become a visible target.

I nudged Fab and pointed to the water, the sides widened and so did the depth. I whispered, "There's a little room to stay close to the bank for the next few feet, or we take cover in the center and hang on to the skinnier trunks." The further we went the more foliage filled in the dense spots. "She won't be looking for us to swim out." My skin crawled knowing I'd be immersed up to my neck. I went first. My only solace was that the gnats apparently couldn't swim, although they were replaced by larger, louder bugs.

Fab shuddered, sinking down and holding my Glock in the air above the waterline.

"Once it gets dark, if we're not dead, we shimmy over the fence"—I pointed—"and hope the neighbor doesn't have dogs."

"Do you notice how quiet it's gotten?" Fab nudged. "Nothing after the second random spray."

I groaned. "No phone. I left it in my pocket."

Fab turned me around, my back to the bank. She leaned in and whispered, "We're going to get out of this. Now no talking so we can listen for any movement." She stood next to me shoulder to shoulder, and covered her face to ward off bugs.

I blew out a silent huff of air, hoping we wouldn't be here long. I had no idea how long we'd been here already but I'd had enough. I didn't want to die in some

211

hell-hole swamp. I turned my thoughts to my shower at home—the super-duper showerhead, continuous clean water, and sweet-smelling soap.

"Madison Westin," grouched a voice over what sounded like a bullhorn. "If you're hiding in the bushes now would be the time to let us know you're okay."

"That your friend?" Fab shot off a round in the air, letting them know our location.

"Come out with your hands up and no damn gun," Harder bellowed.

We both climbed up the embankment and when my foot slipped and I slid backward, Fab jerked on my arm and held tight, helping me to the top. It had been a lot easier to jump in than the reverse trip. We were both covered in mud, slime, and stringy green debris, which all was strangely more revealing than a wet T-shirt contest.

"Mud's good for the skin," I said.

Fab handed me my Glock and I reholstered it into the back of my wet skirt. "Ready for the perp walk?" She held her hands in the air. "I'm doing it now so no one has an excuse to shoot first, ask questions later."

"You need to figure out how we can make this Brick's fault and bill him triple."

"How are we going to get in the Hummer without ruining the seats?" Fab looked at her lower torso.

"I bet Violet will let us shower and borrow some clothes."

Fab laughed. "Let's get drunk."

"Great idea."

Chapter 32

Fab and I drove home in silence. Fab had even driven the speed limit. I second guessed myself, thinking I should have put a bullet in Violet's head and hoped the guy couldn't get a shot off, and if he did, hoped he couldn't hit anything.

"We'll go through the back and use the outdoor shower. You first," I said to Fab. "I've got beach towels stored in the deck box." I felt bad for her. She looked bedraggled and hollow-eyed. It's hard to stare into the eyes of someone who wants to shoot you—or in her case, inject you—knowing the odds were stacked against you. After my shower I planned to gulp down a glass or two of wine to calm the shakes that had taken over my body.

Beach towels in hand, I turned to see Didier lounged against the French doors, staring first at the woman he loved and then at me, an angry look on his face, his mouth a hard line.

"She's had a very bad day. Take good care of her." I handed him a towel.

As soon as Fab turned off the water, he wrapped the towel around her body, smashing his lips to hers and kissed her hard. He scooped her up in his arms and carried her inside. Neither saying a word, he looked at her in a fiercely possessive way that brought tears rolling down my face.

I stood under the outside shower and decided that,

starting tomorrow, it also needed a bigger showerhead. I rinsed the muck from my hair until the water ran clear. I couldn't wait to get upstairs and take a long shower with soap. I sat by the pool, waiting, thinking about everything that had happened, giving as much time as Fab needed to feel clean.

* * *

Violet turned out to be a cunning psychopath, slipping back into her little girl persona once more when she'd gotten handcuffed for a ride to the police station for formal interrogation. Her version of the story was that Fab and I were responsible for the dead bodies. Without the intervention of Harder, Fab and I would be sitting in a jail cell. Thank goodness he showed up and we had someone in law enforcement who believed us. Kevin and Johnson showed up first, representing local jurisdiction. Johnson stood gleefully, waiting for us to show our faces, salivating to slap on the cuffs. Fab's and my guns were accounted for and logged in as evidence, proving neither of us shot the two dead men. I pointed out to Harder the syringe that Violet had dropped, certain when tested it would show only her fingerprints.

Harder told Johnson to 'F off' when he tried to insinuate himself in the conversation. Harder called my attorney, Cruz, and made arrangements for Fab and I to show up in his office for an early morning appointment. He requested that we both shower and have on clean clothes and then laughed at his own joke before retrieving garbage bags from Ivers' garage so that we could cover the seats.

Fab stood mutely at my side, listening to Harder. She didn't contribute anything, but her attitude against him had clearly softened.

Even though Violet had confessed to us her hand in poisoning her father, we were still shocked when Harder confided that the toxicology reports came back from the lab showing ethyl glycol poisoning as the cause of the kidney failure. The results had taken longer than usual since they were short-staffed and had cases backed up. Ivers died of acute liver failure brought on by the ingestion of anti-freeze. In one hundred percent of these cases, the perpetrator is someone who wants to hasten a loved one's or business associate's trip to the afterlife and starts feeding it to them disguised in food or drink due to its sweet taste. One thing is for certain: Ivers had a miserable death.

Harder already had warrants issued to look for containers of the pink liquid and anything else that would keep Violet in prison the rest of her life. She'd be lucky to get life, as Florida was second in the nation for preferring execution.

Harder also told us he planned to charge her with three counts of first-degree murder and a litany of lesser crimes, giving her zero chance at bail. Harder sneered when she requested to call her attorney—who turned out to be none other than Tucker Davis. What Violet probably didn't know was that Tucker's reputation had been built on defending the truly guilty. It would be sad to see Ivers' estate go to the legal bills for the defense of the woman who killed him.

When Harder said those sweet words, "You're free to go," I whispered, "Don't tell Creole about Fab's and my misadventure. He works so hard, why upset him?"

Harder belly laughed. "I won't, but trust me, he'll find out."

I stood up and went into the house, grabbing a glass of wine on my way upstairs. My hair still felt weird, and it was impossible to run my fingers through the ends. Time for a really good shower that included body shampoo and lots of it.

Chapter 33

"To being alive!" Fab, who rarely drank, clinked her mojito to my margarita. "You're the one with the crazy radar, did you have any idea Violet had two personalities?"

We sat out on the deck at Jake's, choosing the corner table so that we could enjoy the sunshine. On the way in, I pushed a bypass button on the juke box, music filling the room without my having to load up on a handful of quarters.

"The pinafore, Mary Jane-clad personality had me fooled."

"Liked her boots." Fab half-laughed.

I waved to Phil, signaling her to put in our food order. "You okay?"

"Feeling not-so-shell-shocked, thanks to Didier. He's not very happy with me. Asked me if either of us had common sense. I told him honestly, you more than me."

I hated that she sat there second-guessing herself. "Snap out of it, Fabiana." I shook my finger. "We're not mind readers. If she hadn't cornered you that day, it would have been another one. No wallowing."

"Thank goodness you can shoot." She smiled. "I've got to start working on you to dispatch the other person straight to their reward and not just wound them."

The cook delivered our food and set down Styrofoam to-go containers. He knew me well. Good thing; he doubled my usual chicken enchilada order.

Fab dumped her food in a container. "I'd rather drink."

I held my hand out. "Give me the car keys. I may just drive you excruciatingly slowly around town."

"I'll hang out the window and scream at traffic. My friends and I did that once in high school and the neighbor felt compelled to call my parents."

"I'm afraid to ask how they took that bit of news." Fab rarely mentioned her family or past in France. I knew she had a strict childhood.

"My father was livid; he practically turned purple. I spent two weeks in my room and after that was not allowed out of the house for a month. They had an image to protect and if I couldn't behave then they'd keep me hidden away."

"I want to hug you right now." I picked at my food, losing interest, and shoved the rest into the container.

"I've been thinking," Fab said.

I groaned.

"Oh, stop. We should go into the animal retrieval business. Less chance of getting shot."

I laughed hard, wiping the tears from my eyes. "You need another drink and then we'll adjourn to the pool. You'll need a nap by then; your good sense will come back."

* * *

I headed down to the docks in Lauderdale, having called Mother and found out that Brad had docked. I'd been waiting on him for a few days. He'd be spending the day cleaning and restocking his boat. I'd been evasive with her, as I wanted to have a little brother/sister time. I wanted some input on Creole before I followed my inclinations, and thought this should be interesting, talking to my brother about my love life.

Brad spent long hours on the water as a commercial fisherman, staying out for long stretches of time until his tanks were stocked with fish. There were lots of grouper in these local waters. I had a fondness for the white fish, preferring it barbequed.

Now that he had a girlfriend and the relationship looked serious, I knew he wanted to cut back on time spent away from home. Julie was the first girlfriend Mother and I actually liked. Only a few had even been tolerable. My brother was a magnet for the unstable ones. Thankfully, he'd broken that pattern. Mother once told me, "It's all about the sex for the first few months and then you better have something to talk about."

I saw my brother standing on the deck of his boat, the wind tossing his sun-bleached hair. Looking healthy with his shirt off, he worked alongside his men and never asked them to do something he wouldn't do. He had a regular crew of men who enjoyed working with him, which made it easy since he didn't have the never-ending parade of misfits. When he turned in my direction, I waved my arm from the window. He didn't notice, but one of his crew members saw me and looked around to see who I was waving to. Finally, he hit Brad on the back and they both waved.

I parked around the corner. The visitor parking lot was blocked off and a sign rolled into the entrance side read, Full. The quickest way back was to cut across a deserted old portion of highway, ducking under the chained off entry and ignoring the Keep Out signs. This part of the docks had a notorious reputation and was known for illegal activities, which I assumed didn't happen in broad daylight with boats of fishermen docked. I'd be damned if I'd walk around. I crossed under an old road that ran overhead and was partially demolished in favor of the newer and shinier twin that had been built alongside it. My brother hung on the rail, watching me, then started to wave again. I waved back and stumbled out of my shoe.

A black Mercedes rolled by me and parked further up. As I bent down, two men climbed out of the back in black trousers, the sleeves of their dress shirts rolled up; both had shoulder holsters, making them look like well-dressed thugs. One man held a briefcase at his side. I crouched behind a cement column. One more step and I'd be standing in the open. Making a run for it was out of the question so I stayed put, hoping not to attract too much attention.

Two other men appeared out of nowhere from the opposite end of the overhang looking like an advertisement for a seedy tropical clothing ad. The man with the briefcase held it up, snapped the locks, and displayed the contents—money, and lots of it by my estimation. I looked around and saw no one else in sight. I got that familiar tingle on my neck which served as a warning not to be ignored. As if I hadn't had enough excitement, I'd bet I was a witness to a major drug buy. The man who stepped forward pushed his sunglasses onto his head, looking suspiciously like Stanhope. Doing a double take, my eyes jerked to his accomplice and I bit my lip to keep from making any noise. Stanhope and Creole were in action. I stayed glued to every second. Knowing drugs and guns were involved, I should have backtracked my way out of the middle of trouble, but instead, I continued to watch the two. Stanhope produced a small knife and sliced through one of the bags. He licked the tip and nodded his head. The duo exchanged briefcases.

An overly large hand clamped down hard against my mouth and hauled me from behind the pole. The three hundred-pound giant jerked me off the ground and shook me like a rag doll. "Look what we have here, boys," he yelled, hoisting me under one arm and carrying me forward.

Sirens blared, coming from every direction. All hell broke loose. I elbowed the giant in his side, he grunted and dropped me to the ground in a heap. Stumbling up, I reached for my Glock but didn't get far, as once again, he jerked me off of my feet in a vise grip and hauled me up under his arm. A dozen black undercover vehicles converged on the area and gunshots rang out, uniforms running everywhere. The big guy pitched me across into the dirt and I curled up next to the fence. Deciding he wasn't done with me, he grabbed me again. Not going down without a fight, I kicked and screamed, making contact with undetermined body parts. My head whipped around by my hair, a mouth smashing down over mine, and I felt the lips move as a voice said, "Shut up."

I recognized the menacing voice and calmed only slightly, wanting confirmation before giving in. I struggled to catch my breath.

Creole gripped my forearm and wrenched me forward. "We've got to get out of here."

Frustrated when I whimpered about my toes being scraped from being dragged, he tossed me over his shoulder and walked so fast I had to grip his shirt. I saw Brad jump off the side of his boat, feet hitting the deck at a run; his crew members stared as I disappeared out of sight. Creole dumped me in the front seat of an old Ford Falcon that looked like it should be at the crusher. It stunned me when the engine caught and sounded in good repair.

Creole got in my face. "What in the hell?" he yelled.

I flinched and closed my eyes, tears trickling out of the corners. "I went to meet Brad," I said softly.

Creole took my face in his hands. "Stop that, now." His thumbs wiped the tears away. "You know I can't handle it when you cry. Why were you walking in an area that had signs posted to keep the hell out?"

"I had to park a couple of blocks away and knew it was a shortcut. You have to get a hold of Brad and let him know I'm okay."

"Stanhope will take care of that." He ran his hands over my arms, lifting my leg, dropping a soft kiss on my scraped knee. "Any other damage I don't know about?"

I shook my head and pointed. "My SUV's parked over there."

"I'll get word to Brad. He'll get it to your house. You won't need it while you're in protective custody."

"What the hell are you talking about?"

"The leader, Ramon Arturo, got away, and as long as he's on the loose, you'll do what I tell you, when I tell you. He knows what you look like and he watched me run to your rescue, so he knows you're important to me and wouldn't hesitate to track you down and kill you in a most unpleasant way. Got it?"

His eyes turned dark blue when he got mad; something told me now wasn't the time to argue. "Where are you taking me?"

"No, damn it. You answer my question and promise that you're going to cooperate," he said, his voice on the rise.

"Okay, I promise. Stop with the yelling and growling." I covered my face with my hands resting on my bent knees. Let him think I was crying, I didn't care.

He rubbed my back. "I was very proud of you back there, kicking and struggling until you forced him to drop you."

I stayed silent for a few minutes trying to figure out where things went wrong. "This really is a crappy car. There's no window handle, what do you do in the rain? The seats are so bad my butt feels like it's banging on the floor, not to mention I can hardly see out the window."

"I'm a drug dealer, remember?"

"Not a very good one, apparently."

"I'm taking you to a safe house, where you will stay put. I'll make sure you have what you need and then I'll have to leave to help track Ramon. I'm trusting that when I come back you'll be right where I left you."

"What kind of stupid program is this? You don't leave witnesses unprotected, I watch enough television to know that some fat guy stands guard and plays cards."

"You're going to pay for driving me nuts. I'm taking you to a house that no one knows about except me and now you."

If his eyes hadn't been smiling at me, the shivers running up my spine might have been those of fear. I entwined my fingers in his. "I'll do my very best to do everything you ask."

He threw his head back and laughed. "When this is over, come away with me—or will you make me kidnap you?"

"You'd force me?"

He ran his finger down my cheek. "A little uninterrupted time and I wouldn't have to."

My cheeks burned red. I turned my face to the window; "uninterrupted time" had me smiling.

He cut through all the seedy areas of town and jumped on the turnpike back to the Keys. I thought he planned to stash me in The Cove somewhere, but he passed up all the exits and headed further south. It surprised me when he got off at Hibiscus Key, which I assumed was nothing more than a turn-around for those going the wrong direction. A few feet ahead he veered off the pavement and onto a dirt road that wound its way toward a wall of trees where the road became paved again, curving around, hugging the water, passing an occasional house that didn't look lived in. The smell of the ocean had me breathing deeply. I realized that I felt content and safe with Creole, knowing he'd never let anything happen to me. At the end of the road, he parked in the driveway of a welcoming beach cottage that sat perched over the edge of the water.

Chapter 34

"It's so beautiful and quiet out here." I looked around in awe, watching the egrets stroll the beach looking for food. As soon as the car engine died, the sounds of the water splashing against the rocks could be heard along the stretch of pristine white sand that discouraged visitors, forbidding parking on the street. "Whose house is this?" I followed him to the front door.

Creole inserted a key in the lock, and scooped me off my feet, carrying me inside, kicking the door closed. "Mine."

The one room open floor plan had an unobstructed view of the water through a solid wall of sliding glass pocket doors that opened onto a patio, complete with swimming pool, that overlooked the Gulf.

"Are you going to put me down? Give me a tour?" I asked.

He slid my body down the front of his until my toes touched the floor and I thought I'd catch fire. He captured my mouth in his, and my lips slightly parted as I inhaled a shivered breath. I wanted his kiss as much as he wanted mine.

He grabbed my forearms and pushed me back. "Enough. I have to go."

"Don't take this off." I ran my hands under his shirt, feeling up his bulletproof vest.

He took me into the kitchen with its bamboo

cabinetry and flooring, granite countertops, and top-of-the-line appliances. "Since I know you're a wiz with the microwave, you won't go hungry with what's in the freezer." He opened the door to an impressive pantry and pulled out a can of my favorite coffee, setting it onto the counter. "I plan ahead."

I hugged him hard. "So I don't go near the windows, what else?"

"Don't go out of this house, except for the patio area. No calls, which is why I'm keeping your phone." He opened the drawer where a Smith and Wesson lay next to the can opener. "Just in case. I'll be back in a few hours to check on you."

I fisted my hand in the front of his shirt. "Listen to me very carefully, Mr. Luc Baptiste, a.k.a. Creole, I'll be quite vexed with you if you get hurt."

"That reminds me," he said, as he picked me up and carried me into the bathroom, setting me onto the toilet seat. He opened the cabinet and took out some peroxide and cotton balls, and kneeled down onto the floor and cleaned my knee.

He looked so serious it amused me. "Thank you for rescuing me," I said as I ran my fingers through his messy hair, kissing the top of his head.

"When I heard you scream I wanted to kill that gorilla-looking bastard," he growled.

When he finished playing doctor, he kissed my owie and I sighed, wishing both knees had been scrapped. "This house is amazing." The claw-foot tub faced the window; even the bathroom had a view, along with a walk-in shower that had room for four with multiple showerheads coming from all directions.

"I hired a contractor for the outside, but did the work on every square inch of the interior myself. This is my hideaway and it needed to be comfortable."

"I'm impressed." On the way into the bathroom we had passed a king-sized bed that sat tucked behind a double screen. It, too, enjoyed the same incredible water view.

He wrapped his arms around my middle and carried me to the couch, laying his head against my stomach. "My house is your house, so make yourself comfortable. Don't forget your promise."

"I don't want you to go. You know how you don't like it when I get hurt, well I won't like it if you come back to me with so much as a scratch. All those cops and you couldn't shoot the bad guys?"

"It makes my job easier if they're hauled in alive so we can squeeze information out of them about friends and associates. Don't worry about me. I'll be back in a few to check on you." He kissed me chastely on the lips and left.

The door closed softly and the silence engulfed me. It felt weird to be out in the middle of nowhere by myself with a very long walk to the main road.

I prowled around the house for a while, and then stood on the deck admiring the view. Sucking in the salty air, the steadiness of the Gulf waters calmed my nerves. I knew that if I didn't think of something fast, I'd break my promise and walk back to town, hiding out at the funeral home—at least I'd have someone to talk to. The only thing that stopped me, Creole angry was more than likely akin to controlling a wet cat.

Since I'd been told to treat this as my own house, I snooped through every cupboard. Creole had excellent taste. I never took baths but today would be the exception. I helped myself to the thickest bath towel I'd ever run my hand over, a cigar, dish soap, and a bestselling thriller novel from ten years ago that I found. I'd seen the movie, but everyone knows the book is always better.

I filled the tub with water and got a little carried away with my makeshift bubbles. Thank goodness he had decent lotion in the cabinet for what would be my dried out, pruney skin. The man thought of everything. I sighed, leaning back against a large bath pillow, not one of the squatty ones that barely supported one's neck.

If this were my bathroom, I'd rethink my bathing ritual. It felt indulgent to sit in piles of bubbles, cigar hanging out of my mouth, looking out over the water, music blaring in from the living room. I forgot all about the book and dozed off, one leg hanging over the side so I didn't slip in and drown.

My foot twitched as something large crawled across the bottom. I jerked upright and screamed, kicking water all over the window and floor, my eyes flying open.

"Don't kick me in the face." Creole grabbed my ankle, easing me back into the water.

"Shouldn't you knock or something?" I sputtered.

"I don't knock at your house. Besides, who could hear with the music turned up full blast? Good thing I don't have neighbors." He took the sponge and ran it up my leg. "I'd be happy to bathe all the hard to reach places." He stared at the water as though he could see through the bubbles.

I blushed and my body tingled. I changed the subject. "What's the update?"

"We've got someone working on Ramon's exact

location now, and once we narrow the coordinates, the bust goes down tonight." He picked the cigar up off the floor. "You ruined a perfectly good cigar and didn't even light it?" He looked at the dish soap. "Remind me to put real bubble bath on my grocery list."

"I don't smoke!" I took the cigar from his hands and put it in my mouth. "Hand me the book." I hung my leg back over the tub. "I'm feeling pretty decadent in this sexy bathtub."

He groaned and picked up the sponge again.

"If you'll close the door on your way out, I'll be out in a minute."

I slapped on his lotion and wrapped myself in a terrycloth robe, pulling the belt tight. I smiled in the mirror, happy he came back so quickly and in one piece.

Creole lay across the bed. "I like my favorite robe on you. Come kiss me, I have to leave."

"You just got here," I whined. "Promise me, same as before, you'll be careful." I shook my finger at him moving to the edge of the bed.

"I promise I'll be here when you wake up." He pulled me down next to him. Our lips collided in a ruthless kiss. He groaned and ran his tongue against me, urging my mouth open as he deepened the kiss, toying with my tongue and biting my lips until I was breathing hard, longing for more. He drew back, hooking one of my fingers into his mouth, and sucked. Then brought my hand to his lips and placed a lover's kiss on my palm.

* * *

Last night had been a complete bore, cut off from the

outside world. I brooded, deeply in phone withdrawal. I missed the constant stream of people in and out of my house. The television only had local channels, and there was no laptop—it had been hard to entertain myself. I double checked the door locks, read, and then left the television on with the sound down for company.

I had my morning coffee and breakfast, made the bed, and paced the floor watching the clock. Where in the hell was he? He said when I woke up, not hours later. Creole wouldn't leave me waiting, he knows I'd do something rash. Yesterday I found a change jar while snooping. I helped myself to the paper money and left an IOU note. I grabbed a cloth grocery bag that still had the "Congratulations, you're a winner" sticker attached, threw in three bottles of water, and hoped the walk to the road wasn't as long as I remembered.

I loved his house and really liked the idea that he hadn't brought another woman to share the view. I daydreamed about sitting out on his deck, sharing breakfast, and doing something as mundane as talking about our day and enjoying every moment.

It had been a healthy hike to the main road, and sucking down one bottle of water, I thought to myself that those long walks on the beach were paying off. I mulled my options; my thumb might very well get me a ride with a weirdo. I couldn't remember how far the next exit that boasted businesses was, and stopping at someone's house might get me the same result as sticking my finger out. I stuck to the far side of the road as cars whizzed by blowing my hair every which way. Hoping to get to civilization before dark, and wondering why the hell Creole hadn't passed me up to turnaround so that he could yell at me, I refused to think anything negative.

Up ahead a sheriff car sat parked, lights flashing. Of all the bad luck, Johnson sat behind the wheel. He lowered the passenger window. "It's dangerous to walk alongside the road."

I started to say something and noticed that the car in front belonged to Tropical Slumber. Before I could step away, Johnson called me back. "This is official business, I suggest you move along."

"I know the owners of the funeral home. I'm just trying to get back to The Cove or the next town where I can use a phone."

"You're not far. The next gas station is about a mile up the road." The window went back up.

I walked past the Cadillac. Dickie had the visor down and was playing with his hair while looking in the mirror. I stepped in front of the car where Dickie saw me and waved. I stuck my thumb out.

Johnson's eyes bore into me as he approached the driver-side window. "No hitchhiking," he yelled and pointed to the sign.

I had tired of brisk-walking, my feet preferred to shuffle now. I glanced over my shoulder constantly, not able to walk backward because it made me nauseous. Finally, Johnson got in his car and drove around Dickie. Before he could drive off, I ran back. Dickie got out and opened the door, always the gentleman.

"Please, oh please, give me a ride home. I'll owe you a favor." I turned slightly but couldn't see in the back.

"I'll give you a ride home and no favor needed, what kind of person would do that? Don't worry, there's no one else but the two of us, dead or alive," he laughed.

Must be funeral humor. "Any breaking news I should know about?"

"I bet you've got a good story—no car, walking, inquiring about the news. Just a few drunks we know, getting into fights. Are you going to tell me?" he asked.

"I can't now, but I'll share when I can." If the story were only about me, I'd tell him. I trusted Dickie, but with others involved, it was not my story to tell.

"Butch quit. Good thing, we wanted to fire him without a confrontation. Took the Cad and had it detailed on the inside." Dickie shook his head. "We hired a nice older gentleman."

"Will you drop me at the main beach parking? I'll walk the rest of the way. Don't tell anyone you saw me."

His dark eyes clouded over. "If you're in trouble, we'll hide you at the funeral home."

"You and Raul have certainly become good friends." I got out after he took a space in the far corner. "Thank you." I waved and sprinted across the sand and down to the water.

Chapter 35

Coming in the back way, I noticed the patio doors were closed so, not having a lock pick handy, I got out the hide-a-key. I called out, but no one answered. I picked up Jazz and hugged him until he meowed. I took him upstairs with me, where I sat him on my bed, next to my purse. That was nice of someone. My replacement phone sat on top, dead, and I plugged it in while taking a shower. The phone company had it replaced within twenty-four hours with a lecture that insurance didn't cover the carelessness of throwing it in the water. I thanked her and asked when my contract would expire and made a note to switch companies.

My first phone call was to Harder. I wanted to hear Creole's voice but didn't want to be a distraction on his case either.

"Where are you?" he asked. It surprised me that he saved me as a contact.

"Creole promised to check in this morning and I haven't heard from him. Just need to know he's okay."

"I didn't know where he had you stashed or I would've come for a visit myself. Creole's in the Tarpon Cove hospital."

I shrieked. "Is he going to be okay? I have to go." I hung up and grabbed my purse, running downstairs.

My phone rang several times, but I left it unanswered until I skidded out of the driveway.

"Don't you ever hang up on me again," Harder yelled. "I'll arrest you."

"Tell me he's not going to die." I cut over to a side street, knowing the route the ambulance used to avoid traffic.

"He got shot, but it's not life threatening. He took a tumble off a second floor parking structure. An awning broke his fall but when he rolled off, he bumped his head and he's in a coma. It's not as bad as it sounds; he's showing signs of coming around any time now."

"Did you get the drug lord?"

"Him and three of his bodyguards. One is in the hospital. We're going to amp up the pressure on that one for information."

I pulled into the parking lot, irritated that the pedestrians I just braked for seemed to be taking their sweet time. "I'm at the hospital, so I'm hanging up on you now, okay?"

"Talk to you later."

I ran into the hospital, slowing to a walk when I got to the nurse's desk, happy to see Shirl. "Where is he?" I asked, out of breath.

"I suppose you mean Creole." She smiled. "He's got a corner cubicle in intensive care but hospital rules, family only."

I looked her straight in the eye. "We're cousins. He's not by himself, is he?"

"He sure doesn't look at you like family, unless you folks don't object to inbreeding. He's getting top-rated nursing care. Creole's aunt, you know, your mother, is quite the pain in the…you'll find out. Thank goodness Brad showed up with his kid and took her to dinner."

"I'll call them after I see Creole. Do I really need to make threats? Because I will." I stared her down.

"You can be really annoying. If anyone asks, you're his sister." Shirl motioned me to follow her down the hall. "I'll note it on his chart."

"Tell me he's going to fully recover?" I hustled to match her long-legged stride.

Shirl escorted me through intensive care to the far side where she waved to two nurses behind the counter. She led me to a cubicle in the far corner, which in actuality was a smaller version of a hospital room.

Creole lay in the big hospital bed hooked up to machines, letting people know his body functions were in the normal range. He had gauze wrapped around his head, two gigantic black eyes, and bruises on the rest of his face and on the one arm not covered by the blanket.

"Please, Shirl. I know visiting time is limited in here but do what you can to make me the exception and I'll give you free rent for a month." I covered his hand with mine, and lightly kissed his cheek and then his lips, disappointed his eyes didn't fly open like in those fairy tales I loved as a kid.

"Don't think I won't milk this situation to my benefit," she said. "Free food at Jake's for the nurses?"

I nodded my head. "I won't make any trouble."

"You bet your sweet ass you won't. You be quiet, stay out of the nurse's way when they come through on their regular rounds, and make no demands. Keep your mother under control. I'll be back later. I'm on the schedule tonight."

I put my phone on vibrate, sure it would start ringing after people realized I resurfaced.

I brushed Creole's hair from his face and whispered in his ear, "Wake up, right now, damn you. You don't get to save my life and die." I dragged a chair next to his bed, and held his hand. "Should I start talking until you can't take it anymore and you have to open your eyes to get rid of me?"

"I could take shameful advantage of you." I giggled at the thought, embarrassing myself. I ran my hand over his cheek. "Who'd know? And maybe if I woke one part of you up, the rest of you would be eager to be in the real world again."

"How's the food here?" I asked.

He didn't answer.

"I want to call Brad and have him bring me dinner but I'm not sharing visitation time. If they know I'm here, they'll hurry back." I laid my face on his stomach. "You're not very talkative."

The door opened. "You can't call a girlfriend? I had to find your purse and car gone to know," Fab hissed.

"How did you get in?"

"I'm family. Don't look at me like that, I told them I was his sister." She leaned over Creole. "Wake the hell up," she hissed in his ear.

I gave her a dirty look. "Miss me?"

"Well, kinda. Didier had to go to New York. Just me and my cat and when Creole got brought in, your mother, Brad, Julie, and Liam."

"Will you be a best friend and get me some take out from Jake's?"

"I wouldn't want you to miss out on yummy hospital food. I'll stay with him while you run down to the restaurant, it's on the bottom level." She half-smiled.

236

"While you're gone, I'll peek under that ugly hospital gown. Or have you done it already?"

My mouth dropped. "He's in a coma!"

Fab shook her head. "I'll do it."

I moved between her and Creole, forcing her to step back. "You will not!"

"A little possessive for someone you're not interested in," she said, and smirked.

"How's Mother?" I asked.

"Before he got shot, he was the one to explain to her that he had you in hiding. She flipped. Then he took her outside, they talked, and when they came back in she had calmed down. I would've given anything to eavesdrop on that conversation. Brad grumbled big time that he can't get her to do what he tells her. She's been here the whole time, issuing orders, hardly allowing anyone to visit. She needs to go home and get some sleep."

"They have a great relationship. I know he takes her to lunch or dinner at least once a week, in between chasing bad guys. She told me he picks the best little cafes, they're always trying new food."

The nurse appeared in the doorway. "One of you will have to leave. His mother is back. Only two visitors at a time."

I rolled my eyes. "Next thing you know Didier will be a long-lost brother."

We both laughed.

"I'm going home," Fab said. "If I don't see you tonight, I'll be back in the morning."

"Did he wake up?" Mother asked a minute later.

I shook my head. "Not yet," I said, running my fingers across his cheek.

She hugged me. "Are you okay?" She looked me over. "I don't understand what happened. No one will tell me a damn thing. Why were you on the docks? Why did Creole have to hide you? Were you involved?"

"You make it sound like somehow this is all my fault. You know what he does for a living."

"I did think maybe it was a stupid Brick case where everyone gets hurt," she said.

"I went to the docks to meet Brad and the rest you'll have to ask Creole when he wakes up. I'm going to go say hello to Brad."

Liam hugged me the second I walked into the waiting room. "Take Mother home, and tell her she needs to sleep or something," I said to Brad. "She's dead set against a relationship between me and Creole and just asked me if I had anything to do with him getting shot."

"I talked to her about that and told her if she didn't want to damage her relationship between the two of you, she'd better mind her own business. She's worried you're on the rebound. I reminded her that you were the most supportive of her relationship with Spoon. Hell, I only tolerate the guy."

Phil walked in and extended a brown bag to me. "Boss lady's favorites are in here. I offered to drop it by on my way home."

"I'm so starving. Have you met my brother and his kid, Liam?"

Liam gave Brad a big smile. It pleased me to see them so happy together. Watching my brother with Liam proved he'd be a great dad. I had to keep from laughing when Brad looked over the long-legged Phil in an appreciative way and Liam, watching, mimicked him.

They exchanged a few sentences of small talk while I ate. Phil waved and left.

"I about had heart failure when I saw Creole and Stanfield, and tried to wave you off," Brad said. "I chased down Stanfield, who told me that you were there to see me. Why would you cut through Drug Corner and not go around? There is never a good time of day to be in that area. What did you want? It must have been important, since you never meet me at my boat."

"I wanted brotherly advice about Creole and Mother. Next time, I promise no more short cuts."

He pulled me to him, hugging me tight. "I like him better than the last one. I'll get Mother out of here so you can spend time with him."

I winked. "I'm going to stay here and eat until you make it happen."

Brad forced Mother to leave when he found her dozed off on her cupped hands.

Liam got a text from Brad to meet them outside. Neither one of them stopped to say good-bye. Mother would have a fit if the high-heel was on the other foot and I treated her in that dismissive fashion.

Chapter 36

I went back to Creole's bedside and laid a big kiss on him. Someone had moved the chair over into the corner and I pushed it back next to the bed. I laced my fingers in his. If he woke up, I wanted to be the first to know. I laid my head on the mattress. It didn't take long for my shoulders to ache. I checked out the nursing area, which was quiet since none of the other patients had visitors. The lights had been dimmed, except where two nurses sat shuffling through paperwork.

I closed the door quietly and walked around to the far side of the bed, slipped off my shoes, and climbed in next to Creole. Thank goodness for sweat pants—my butt would be on display in a skirt. I pulled his arm around me, nestling my face against his side and went to sleep.

I jerked awake whispering, "Creole?"

"No, it's not your cousin," Shirl huffed, continuing to hit my shoulder. "You can't jump in bed with comatose patients."

"It's not like I did anything." I sat up on the edge of the bed.

"Go in the lounge and take a nap. I'll call you if anything changes," Shirl said.

Tears trickled down my face. "No, I'm not going anywhere."

Shirl handed me a Kleenex. "I'll be back before rounds are made just ahead of shift change. If you get

240

caught again don't tell anyone you know me."

I whispered in his ear, "Wake up, please." I lay my head back down and went right back to sleep.

* * *

During shift change, I went home and showered, stopping for a caramel latte on the way back to the hospital. I sipped it slowly by Creole's bedside. He squeezed my hand and I damn near spilled my coffee before I set it aside and jumped out of the chair. His eyes fluttered open and I hit the button by the bed. The nurse appeared instantly.

She took over, checking his vitals, talking to him, and smiling. "He's coming around. He might be a little disoriented, and most first requests are for water." She picked up the little yellow pitcher and rinsed it out in the bathroom, refilling it.

I refrained from spouting my personal commentary on tap water and made a mental note to sneak in bottled water. The nurse leaned over him and he opened his eyes again, this time looking down her hospital top, which had two buttons undone, and stared at her ample breasts. She filled his cup and held the straw to his lips. He took a long drink and smiled at her.

I moved out of the corner to the bed. "I'll do that."

"Talk to him; be nice, but not too nice." She smirked. "I'll check back every few minutes."

Mother walked in and kissed his cheek. "I brought you a fresh apple muffin." She held up the bag, setting it on the tray table.

"He's coming around," I said. "We're supposed to

talk to him."

Mother started telling him about her latest fishing trip with Spoon and how she didn't catch anything. The doctor came in and ordered us to leave. We both walked silently to the waiting room.

"I can see you have feelings for Creole, Madison. I just want you to make sure that he's what you really want before acting, so neither of you gets hurt," Mother said.

Why don't you fix me up again, sat on the tip of my tongue, *since that's gone so well in the past*—but I held on to my anger. "What you should be worried about is Creole falling for someone who hates our family, like Brad has done in the past. There were long periods of time that we didn't see him very much. Lately, it feels like you're more concerned about his feelings than mine."

"Spoonie told me I should mind my own business and I wished I'd taken his advice. That's about the third time lately I wish I'd listened to him."

I looked down and scrunched my face. *Spoonie!* "You should tell him you're going to start listening to him. That makes boyfriends happy."

"He's coming by to pick me up for lunch now that Creole's awake, or almost, anyway."

If Shirl had been on duty I'd have tracked her down by now to find out what the doctor was doing.

Mother interrupted my worries. "Where did Creole hide you?"

"A safe house. I've been sworn not to divulge the location. Didn't take me long to realize I didn't like being away from family and friends."

The nurse stuck her face in the door. "Mr. Creole

is awake. He requested to see the redhead."

I flew down the hall, slowed upon entering the intensive care unit, and walked quickly to his cubicle. I leaned over, holding my lips to his, kissing him softly.

"Don't cry," he said, sounding raspy.

I brushed his dark hair out of his face, staring into his crystal blue eyes. "I'm very annoyed with you," I said sternly. "You broke your promise not to get hurt." I nipped his earlobe.

"Dreams of bubble baths, cigars, and a redhead kept me going."

My cheeks burned and I held the straw to his dry lips, intently watching him drink.

"You're awake," Mother said from the doorway. She kissed his cheek. "Have you thought about selling insurance?"

* * *

Creole spent one more day in intensive care and got transferred to his own room, which was a good sign that he'd be released soon. During that time, he had several visits from "dark, disreputable looking men," according to Shirl, who said they showed up in the wee hours of the morning claiming some vague familial relationship.

I snuck up behind the guy named Help during one such early dawn visit, after returning from showering and changing my clothes.

"What the hell are you doing, sneaking up on me?" he demanded. He sported a few days of beard growth, dark clothing, and dark glasses; how he could see I don't know, with his baseball cap pulled down so low.

He was the picture of a street-corner he-whore looking for someone to rob.

I ignored his question. "What's your real name or alias? How can I introduce you as Help?"

"None of your business, and I don't want to meet anyone."

"Fine." I gave him a snooty look right back. "There must be someone I can complain to about your bad attitude."

"Trust me, this job requires no personality."

"If I invited you to a barbeque, would you come?"

He stared at me, laughed, and hit the bar on the entrance door to the hospital, disappearing. The morning light threatened to break through the clouds.

Chapter 37

A frantic call from Shirl had me racing to the hospital. "Your mother is here pressuring the doctor to release Creole so she can take him to her house to recuperate. He doesn't want to hurt her feelings; he wants you to do it."

I sighed. "Mother is really good at playing nurse, a lot more nurturing than I'll ever be."

Shirl snorted. "Your hot boyfriend—cousin, whatever—wants you to get your pretty little ass over here now. His words, not mine. And he yelled, 'Now.'"

Creole looked miserable sitting in a chair and struggling to put his shoes on, while Mother talked his ear off. I wanted to laugh but I didn't.

"Mother," I said, putting my hands on my hips. "Here are the reasons why Creole is coming home with me and I know you want the best for him."

She didn't look happy, but not mad either.

"We have three adults at my house. Didier is equal in size to Creole to assist him, better than you or me. I can get a doctor to make a house call with the push of a button and a pretty please. While he's recuperating, his scurvy associates will be able to come and visit. They won't go to Coral Gables."

"I suppose you're right about Didier, I did think about what I'd do if something happened." She wagged her finger at Creole. "I'll be bringing my homemade soup."

I knelt down in front of Creole and picked up his foot, running my nails across the bottom and over his ankle, sitting it in my lap. I slid on the tennis shoe he'd been struggling with, tying the laces. He put his other foot in my lap, and I raked my nails up the back of his leg before tying that shoe. Creole had one hand in my hair, holding the back of my head, flexing his fingers, his blue eyes devouring me.

Mother coughed. "I'll go ask the nurse what's taking so long."

The door closed. Creole leaned forward and I rose up to meet his lips, and we kissed.

I stood up. "There is one more thing. You agree to stay at my house and there will be no whining or complaining. You'll stay until you can walk upstairs without assistance and sneak past Fab into my bedroom." I wagged my finger. "Don't think I won't use my trump card to get you to behave. If you break my rules I'll pack you off to Coral Gables to recuperate under Mother's watchful eye."

I saw in his eyes that had been an effective threat. We both knew she would smother him to death and be bossy.

He ran his thumb across my lips. "It could be months."

"Shh, don't tell Fab."

* * *

Fab and Didier rearranged the furniture and moved the guest bed that never got used against the wall in the living room. I splurged on Egyptian cotton sheets, a down duvet, and lots of pillows. From this vantage point, Creole could easily shoot someone coming in the front door or through the French doors. Jazz had already laid claim to his spot, curled up asleep on a pillow in the corner next to the wall.

"Don't get any ideas." I narrowed my eyes at Creole. "The cat sleeps with me."

"How does that work when you're, uh, you know?"

"Jazz doesn't care for the moving around, so he jumps on the chair and watches. Now lay down, you need to rest." I stood in front of him, pointing to the mattress.

He sat and pulled me onto his lap. "Are you going to undress me?" He held his arms up.

The clothes Creole came into the hospital with had disappeared. Shirl said they probably got trashed, only leaving him with a pair of shoes. I purchased a pair of sweat shorts and shirt for him to make the trip to my house.

"You're not going naked." I frowned at him. "Make a list of what you want from your house and I'll go get it, along with anything else you want or need." I got off his lap.

"You know what would get me better faster?"

"No it won't." I started for the kitchen before he could grab me. "Would you like something to drink?"

Fab and Didier came back from the beach. She threw herself on Creole and gave him a loud smooch on his lips. "How's my much older brother?"

"You better not hurt him," I said.

Didier pulled Fab to him, putting his arm around her. "Don't maul what's mine," he said to Creole.

"How are we going to survive all these A-type

247

personalities under one roof, and I'm the only calm one?" I asked.

They laughed at me.

"Don't you mean five? I'd wager your mother will be here soon with a carload of takeout boxes," Fab said.

"Fab, we have a new rule," I told her.

"What?" Her eyes narrowed. "And why do I have the feeling it only applies to me?"

"Look before you shoot. If someone strolls in looking like a street dealer in a tropical shirt, they're probably a friend of his." I pointed to Creole. "No shooting Harder either or threatening him."

Didier looked down at her and smiled, enjoying that she'd like to unleash a tirade on me.

"Sometimes you squeeze every little bit of fun out of everything," she sniffed.

Someone started kicking the front door; Fab and I looked at each other. "Mother," we said in unison. Fab and Didier went to help her, since everyone knew she overdid the take-out food.

I sat next to Creole. "I hope you're ready for all this togetherness."

He laughed. "I forgot to tell you, a nurse told me an interesting story. She said while I was in a coma you got in my hospital bed and forced yourself on me."

I covered my face in embarrassment. "I didn't," I giggled. "But I thought about it."

Enjoy a preview of the next *Paradise* novel,
Book Six
Coming Soon, Fall 2014

REVENGE
IN PARADISE

DEBORAH BROWN

Chapter 1

The dark grey clouds seemed oppressively heavy. The sun peeped through the rain-laden clouds as they rolled east out into the Atlantic and a rainbow spread across the sky. The emerald-turquoise water surrounded the highway on both sides of the Keys for as far as the eye could see. Palm trees with spindly trunks and long branches lined the far edges of the beach, interspersed with colorful tropical plant life. I rolled down the window and a gentle breeze blew through my long red hair and tousled it into an unruly mess.

I sighed when we veered off the Overseas Highway into Tarpon Cove and pulled up in front of Jake's Bar; yellow crime scene tape was laid across the driveway. An assortment of law enforcement vehicles filled the street. The bomb squad had turned out, outfitted in riot gear, the local fire department and sheriffs pushed to the side in favor of their more illustrative counterparts. Several K-9 dogs patrolled the property in bulletproof vests, sniffing every square inch of the property. My employees filed out of the building in a single line, their hands in the air. Mother looked frazzled, her blonde bob wind-whipped, and the ever-cool-under-pressure Fab was behind her. Both of them were cuffed and each had their own police escort.

I peered through the passenger-side window, "Somehow this will be my fault," I said to Creole.

He squeezed my hand, "I'll give you a written excuse. You've been with me for the last five days."

"Shh, you need to get my story straight. I've been at my childhood friend, Marcy's wedding in Myrtle Beach."

He shook his head, "I don't understand why you didn't just go ahead and tell your family you left town to take your cousin on a sexual test drive."

My Aunt Elizabeth willed all of her colorful friends to me. It turned out she'd known Creole long before I did. He'd been neighbors with my aunt growing up and she had loved him like a son and now so did my mother. His real name is Luc Baptiste, but when you're an undercover detective you get a street name, so we keep his real identity a secret. He had been as close as family before we started sneaking around.

I groaned, "Some people would hear that and think, 'that's why she's so weird,' then begin the inbreeding jokes."

"What kind of trouble have those two gotten into now?" he laughed.

"Can I get another kiss? Who knows when we'll get another chance? This looks like a long afternoon." I stuck my hand under his T-shirt and ran my nails up his chest.

It still amazed me that I'd finally agreed to having a relationship with him. The words barely left my lips before he rushed me out of town for a week on the beach in Key West. We never left the hotel room for the first two days, opening the door only to room service. My favorite moment was on the last day. He took me to a secluded spot on the beach on the pretext of a picnic and swimming and we spent the afternoon entangled in each other's arms surrounded by nature's beauty.

Creole's blue eyes sparkled with amusement, pulling into a parking space in front of the trailer court I had recently acquired. "I don't recognize a single officer. I'll give Harder a call; he can get us a quick update."

Chief Harder of the Miami Police Department is Creole's boss. Their relationship extended outside the office and they always had each other's back. Harder and my relationship had improved considerably from when he thought I was criminal. He helped me on several occasions and I returned the favor whenever he asked.

I ran my fingers through Creole's shoulder-length black hair, pulling his face to mine, "I had a great time."

We both jumped at the pounding on the window.

"What in the hell?" Creole yelled.

Professor Crum glared at him, "I'm having you towed," he snarled.

I threw open the passenger door and slid off the seat of Creole's black over-sized pickup and onto the ground, managing to keep my sundress covering my butt.

"You have anyone towed off my property and I'll evict your old ass. No court hearing," I said, "just a special friend or two to tie you up and deliver you to Minnesota."

"Didn't see you there, girly. Who's he?" Professor Crum stood ramrod-stiff, with his usual good posture, dressed up in his cowboy boots and boxer shorts, his white hair sticking up on end.

"Her boyfriend," Creole growled. "If you ever look at her like that again, I'll blacken both your eyes and I won't care if you're one hundred."

"And to think, you could've had me," Crum

3

winked. "Too late; I'm taken. Got a new lady. We're going out to dinner."

Creole threw his head back and laughed.

I bit my lip; he'd clearly usurped the title of most colorful tenant. "Is that why you're dressed up? I found out your first name is Ernest—or do you prefer Ernie?"

Crum's eyes turned to dark slits and said, "You do not have my permission to call me anything but Professor or Crum."

Crum's condescension didn't bother me anymore since he looked down his nose at everyone.

"What's going on at the bar?" I asked.

"Your mother and that delicious French girl opened the back room for poker. I don't know if they couldn't keep their mouths shut or what, but word spread like a sex disease," he then pulled a condom from the back of his boxers. "I never leave home without one of these babies. I sew pockets on the back of my nice shorts." He turned, wiggling. The pocket turned out to be a piece of mismatched material, this one a piece of a red bandana hand-sewn in place with sloppy stitches.

Creole's phone rang and he stepped away to answer.

"I haven't been gone long enough for them to commit felonies."

"The cops have been there at least two hours," Crum said. "My opinion: They chased a couple of dirtballs out a few nights ago, and the guys came back to get even, Bistro the loan shark and his sleazy muscle, Jethro. I overheard the hot one threatening to shoot them."

Creole walked up in time to hear. "I know Jethro. I can make sure he never bothers you again."

4

"Let's go see how much bail money is needed."

Crum tossed his head in Creole's direction, "I think you can do better," he said.

I tugged on Creole's hand. "Can you make this go away?"

It was a short walk to the bar; the trailer court sat at the opposite end of the same block and was set back from the highway. Mother and Fab had been separated off to the side, away from the other employees and were not able to communicate amongst themselves without shouting. If I'd summed up the situation correctly, no one would be going anywhere soon because at this point there was more standing around than action.

"I'll call in favors to make sure no one in the Westin family goes to jail—and that includes Fab. Or I'll make sure that they don't stay long," he gave me a wry smile. Creole drug me behind the dumpster for a long, slow kiss. I stretched up his chest, standing on tip toes, a moan escaping, begging for more.

Kevin Cory called out my name. He was almost a family member and I knew he hated that idea. He liked my brother Brad, and approved of him dating his sister Julie, but he thought Mother and I were crazy and unsuitable role models for his teenage nephew, Liam.

When we drove by, I'd seen him questioning Philipa, the bartender. Arms across his chest, he didn't look happy about whatever answers she was giving him. We called the bartender Phil—a second-year law student who dazzled the customers with her bubbly personality, long blonde hair and butt-cheek shorts. I didn't worry about what she'd say.

I heard my name called and turned to see Mother

waving, Fab next to her, sporting an angry scowl. Before I could take a step a female sheriff stepped in front of me.

"No lookers," she said as she pointed to the street, "this is an active investigation."

I checked out her uniform. It turned out she was local; her badge read, 'Tarpon Cove'.

The Cove sat at the top of the Keys, the first small town to greet you upon entering the Overseas Highway and after leaving Miami far behind. We had a small sheriff presence and I knew most of them by name.

"We haven't met—I'm Madison Westin, the owner."

Her eye arched a bit at what I assumed was my not offering a courtesy handshake. Anyone who knew me also knew I didn't observe that nicety, but most people just assumed I was ill-mannered. I disliked the term "germaphobe," but I also hated anything slimy, murky, green, watery, and abhorred all bugs in general.

"I've heard about you," she looked me over, amusement on her face. "I'm Kevin's new partner. Officer Ivyliss Sotolongo but you can call me Ivy."

"Johnson's replacement," I smiled. "I heard he got kicked…or transferred somewhere far from The Cove."

"He had a lot to say about you before he left," she laughed. "It had been his dream to lock up your criminal ass which, to his disappointment, was a wish unfulfilled."

"Do you mind if I speak to my Mother and make sure she's okay? Her health is fragile," I said, and managed to maintain eye contact to sell the blatant lie.

Ivy looked over at Mother, who stared back, "She might want to cut back on the cigars. You can have five minutes."

Mother loved a hand-rolled Cuban cigar, she found a family run store in Little Havana that she frequented often. She'd been to the factory and knew everyone by name.

I didn't want to hear the answer to my next question, fearing the worst—but I asked anyway, "Is she under arrest?"

"It's not my call. But evidence is missing, along with a couple of witnesses, their stories are full of potholes, and did I mention they barely agree on anything?"

Damn!

"Jake's caters to law enforcement; they have a special area in the corner of the back deck, one of the best views in the place. Hope to see you soon."

I walked over to Mother, enveloping her in a hug. "What in the hell," I whispered in her ear. "Brad will flip when you tell him." One thing for certain, I wasn't going to be the one to tell my brother and wanted to be out of town again when he found out.

"He doesn't need to know," she snorted. "It was a huge misunderstanding."

"Mother," I mimicked her no-nonsense voice, "I'm sure it wasn't. Who knows you better than I do?"

I looked at my best friend and roommate and stage-whispered, "You couldn't stay out of trouble for a few days?"

"Get your lawyer on the phone. I'm not up to another trip to the big-girl jail," Fab's dark eyes shot Mother hate-filled looks. "I'm so glad your home. I want details."

"Mother," I continued to whisper, after noticing

Ivy had moved closer. "You're in frail health if anyone asks. You can have a miraculous recovery once we get you out of here."

Mother dabbed her eyes.

"Stop, you don't fool me. What the hell happened?" I shook my head. "The truth, not the cleaned up legal version."

"When Fab and I were on a recovery job, we discussed opening the back room for a friendly game, to a select group of friends. Things didn't go as planned," she sighed.

I snapped around and glared at Fab, "You took Mother to boost a car? Were guns drawn?"

"It was an easy job for a change. Found the BMW at the girlfriend's house, I got in and drove away."

"There is no such thing as an easy recovery job. I'll bet cash there's more to your story."

"I didn't have anyone else," she hissed. "You know I need a driver, all she had to do was follow me to Brick's for the drop-off, what could go wrong?"

Brick Famosa owned a high-end car sales/rental lot, Famosa Motors. I thought he stopped renting to people without a credit and background check, especially when they paid with all cash. But apparently not; he kept Fab and I busy driving all over South Florida recovering cars that failed to be returned.

"You're asking me that with a straight face when ninety-percent of our jobs end up with threats of violence?"

"You exaggerate at ninety-percent," she huffed. "Have you ever tried to tell your Mother her idea is a sucky one? She has voices in her head and only listens to them."

"Since when do all these different agencies show up for an illegal card game?"

"Some jackass called in a bomb scare. They burst through the doors, I wanted to run but got down on my knees, like they told me."

"Officer Ivy informed me that no evidence was found. I'm assuming she meant evidence about the card game. How did you make that disappear? Nice job, by the way."

"I texted Madeline, she took care of it; swept everything off the table into garbage bags and sent the men out the secret back door."

Fab must be mad—she called Mother by her first name.

Mother put her head on my shoulder and said, "I had everything covered since I'd run a couple of practice drills before we opened."

Creole walked up behind us, scooping Mother off her feet into a bear hug. "Since when are you in the habit of ticking off drug dealing pond scum?" he asked.

Kevin joined Ivy, and together they glared in our direction.

I cut in, "Mother, did you give a statement to anyone?" She shook her head in the negative.

"Don't say one word until I get Cruz on the phone." Cruz Campion was a hotshot lawyer I kept on speed-dial for just such occasions.

Creole and I exchanged looks.

"Bistro needed a get out of trouble card for a violation of his parole conditions," he said, "so he concocted an elaborate story about guns, gambling and bomb making."

Fab groaned, "I picked up Bistro's car. The BMW belonged to him."

The jail bus rumbled into the driveway. I recognized it as the one they used for special occasions like drunk-driving check points. I watched as my employees filed on board.

"Break up the love feast, ladies, time to get yourselves a seat." Ivey yelled, advancing on us. She looked at me, "We're going over the bar one more time and unless anything new turns up, you can reopen tomorrow."

"No more questions," Creole advised Ivy. "Everyone one of them is lawyered up."

"All of them?" she asked in astonishment.

I smiled at her, "If you ever need a criminal attorney, Cruz Campion is the best in South Florida. He boasts the whole state."

Kevin, who had stood quietly at Ivy's side, spoke up, "It will be a while before they're released and you're not welcome to hang around."

He grabbed Mother's arm, "You might be my nephew's grandmother one day. Why can't you be a good example and bake cookies or something?"

"I don't need to bake as long as there are bakeries."

ABOUT THE AUTHOR

Deborah Brown is the author of the Paradise series. She lives in South Florida, with her ungrateful animals, where Mother Nature takes out her bad attitude in the form of hurricanes.

Visit her website at
http://deborahbrownbooks.blogspot.com

You can contact her at Wildcurls@hotmail.com

Deborah's books are available on Amazon, Barnes & Noble and most online retailers.

17671869R00154

Made in the USA
Middletown, DE
04 February 2015